The Runaway Heiress

a The Gilded West novella

Harper St. George

Contents

The Runaway Heiress   V

The Gilded West   VII

1.   Chapter One   1

2.   Chapter Two   10

3.   Chapter Three   16

4.   Chapter Four   24

5.   Chapter Five   32

6.   Chapter Six   38

7.   Chapter Seven   48

8.   Chapter Eight   58

9.   Chapter Nine   72

10. Chapter Ten   81

11. Chapter Eleven   87

12. Chapter Twelve   96

13. Epilogue   106

The Copper Heir   110

Also by Harper St. George   124

About the author   127

The Runaway Heiress

By Harper St. George

A forbidden attraction sparks between a captive heiress and the gunslinger tasked with delivering her to her wedding in this prequel novella to Harper St. George's The Gilded West series.

Sophie Buchanan is trapped in a gilded cage. Outwardly, she lives a charmed life as the beloved niece of one of the wealthiest men in Helena, Montana Territory, but beneath her elegant facade lies a burning need for revenge. Her uncle orchestrated the accident that killed her parents so he could gain control of their fledgling mining empire. When he arranges a loveless marriage for her—the final part of his plan to control her fortune—she knows it's time to escape.

Standing between Sophie and freedom is Gray, the rugged gunslinger her uncle hired to guard her. But Gray has secrets of his own and letting Sophie escape will ruin the carefully laid plans that will bring her uncle to justice. As much as he wants her for himself, Gray is bound by duty to give her up...even after a forbidden night together changes everything.

As their worlds collide against the opulence of the wealthiest town in the West, Sophie and Gray are forced to choose between duty and a forbidden love that threatens to destroy them both.

The Gilded West

The Runaway Heiress (novella)

The Copper Heir

The Bastard Heir

The Gilded Lady

Chapter One

Helena, Montana Territory, 1888

Married?

Sophie closed her eyes and prayed that she had heard him wrong. Then she counted to ten in an attempt to dispel the anger she could feel rising within her. Experience had taught her that it was never worthwhile to show anger when her uncle was in one of his moods. And he was in rare form today.

She opened her eyes to see him relaxing in the leather wing-backed chair, gazing at his cigar with a self-satisfied smile curving his lips. Having just delivered the blow orchestrated to finally break her, he had every reason to smile. He crossed his legs and picked up the tumbler of cognac from the marble-topped table beside him and took a sip, seeming to forget she was there and that he had just ruined her life.

She hated him.

"Oncle Jean, perhaps I misheard—"

"*Non*, cherie, you heard me correctly. Your wedding will be next month. Anton and I have already discussed the matter. The specifics can be worked out later. Nothing too large. An intimate gathering will suffice. You'll need to have a gown made, but I'm sure an arrangement can be made with Martine to have it finished in time. There will be no need for a Worth gown for such a small celebration, non? If only your mother hadn't run off to marry that Scot, she would have had a proper gown to pass down to you, but..." His words ended on a sigh.

Sophie refrained from pointing out the Scot had been her father and had her mother not run off to marry him the conversation would be moot.

"Well, what can we do?" her uncle continued. "She did what she did, and I do owe her a debt, do I not? I am here now and not in France, and look at my good fortune." He gestured to the room, with its frescoed ceilings, exotic wood floor and gilt-trimmed furnishing; it was the epitome of excessive opulence. Then his gaze lit on her and he gave the smile she hated: worse than smug, this smile was dead. "And I repay a little of my debt every day."

He meant that he repaid the debt by raising her and her brother. He had become their guardian after her parents' untimely death, which meant that he lived a life of luxury on the wealth generated from their copper mine.

"But Monsieur Beaudin is...is..." *Old. Repulsive. Abhorrent.* Each descriptor was more fitting than the last, she had trouble choosing just one.

"Careful, cherie, he is my dearest friend."

Sophie looked at her uncle in his coat of maroon velvet, his garish neckerchief, his pale skin and graying hair slicked back with pomade, and thought he could have been Monsieur Beaudin sitting there for all the difference there was between them. Many of the ladies in town thought him handsome, but she saw only the evil lurking beneath the surface.

"Oncle, you mistake me. I was merely going to point out that he is too sophisticated for a girl who lacks sophistication. While you have been more than kind to take me in, that is what I am having never left Helena, and one never really strays far from one's roots, no?"

A vein twitched in his temple and she knew her barb had landed. She couldn't check the cowardly impulse to glance at the silver hawk's head of his walking cane where it was propped against his chair. Perhaps it was suicide to remind him that he came from Le Marais, a slum in Paris, but recklessness was as much a part of her nature as this forced deference was foreign to it. Being from the same slum, her mother never would've had a proper wedding gown, anyway.

"Rejoice that I have found a Frenchman willing and gracious

3

enough to overlook your many shortcomings. You will be a good wife to him, Sophie, or you will answer to me for it. Do you understand?"

All pretense of civility had fled, leaving his eyes cold and flat. The look he gave her now was the look that had earned him free rein in the copper mines in this region of the territory. His only rivals were the Jamesons. They had long ago divided the valley and mountain range between them in a precarious agreement that was like a box of dynamite on the verge of ignition.

"Oui. Could I telegraph Alexandre? He should come to the ceremony." She had not seen her brother since he'd been forced to sign over his inheritance. Their uncle had sent him off to Chicago under the guise of educating him. That had been about five years ago, though Jean gave her regular updates.

His good humor restored by her compliance, her uncle smiled and took a puff of his cigar. "I will see that he is notified, but you may write a letter to post if you wish." Finished with the conversation, he said, "The Nelsons' ball is at nine tonight. Be ready."

Sophie stood to take her leave. "Merci, Oncle." It was her customary closing with any of their conversations.

Thank you, Uncle. Thank you for taking me in after you murdered my parents. Thank you for allowing me breath one more day. Thank you for not committing most of the unspeakable crimes against me your soulless eyes promise you are capable of perpetrating.

Yet.

She hated him! If only her life didn't stretch out before her as one endless act devoted to playing out the whims of that monster. Already, the sounds of despair and anger that she'd had trouble containing were threatening to escape her throat, causing her shoulders to shake with the effort of subduing them. She closed the door to his study, intent on fleeing to her room. But when she turned, something solid and decidedly masculine blocked her path.

Without even looking, she knew who it was. Gray. She was always so preternaturally aware of him; every fiber of her being knew when he was near. Today he was Jean's sentry. How had she not noticed him on her way into the study?

Strong hands came up to her waist to steady her. She slowly looked up at him, unable to so quickly hide the wetness in her eyes and the misery lurking behind them.

"Breathe."

His voice poured over her, further igniting the prickling recognition she had no right to feel. It was an awareness that went much deeper than the simple fact that she had heard his voice many times before. Her fingers curled against his strong chest, begging to stroke him, to take some comfort from him, the man she had come to think of as her favorite.

Instinctively, her body did as he commanded. She sucked in a deep breath while allowing her gaze to trace his face and luxuriate in the rare chance to study him. He was stoic, forbid-

5

ding like the rest of her uncle's gunmen, and handsome. Her gaze touched his strong jaw, blade-straight nose, and sculpted cheekbones. There was a touch of brown in his complexion and midnight in his hair which bespoke a native heritage. He was breathtaking. She sometimes wondered if that alone was the reason she was so fascinated by him, but then he would speak and prove her wrong. There was so much more to him.

"Did he hurt you?" His gaze touched every part of her face, leaving her skin hot and tingling where it lingered.

That look was the perfect example of what drew her to him. It was full of genuine concern. He was the only one who looked at her as someone who might be in pain or need help. He gave her a glimpse of what it might be like to feel cared for and safe, even though the very idea of safety was wrong. If Jean ordered any of his men to remove her as a threat, none of them would hesitate. Gray included.

She shivered, reminding herself to never forget that her uncle only employed men he had thoroughly vetted. They were completely loyal to him. But still...she couldn't step away.

"No, he didn't. I'm fine." But then she shook her head because she wasn't fine at all. "I don't know," she answered honestly. The back of her throat ached, and she swallowed past the lump that had formed there.

"Just breathe in." His hands began to lightly stroke up and down the length of her back. Again her body obeyed his command and she took in a deep gulp of air. "Now let it out slowly."

His startling gray eyes held hers as he bid her repeat the process two more times. He was so confident in his soothing commands that the tension began to seep from her body. The feeling of security inexplicably made her confide her trouble to him.

"I'm going to be married. I don't..." But her voice trailed off when his eyes narrowed.

"When?" The question was a breath between them.

"In a month." *Oh, God, only weeks away!* She bit the inside of her lip to keep it from trembling.

For a moment there was nothing, no response, nothing flickering in his eyes. There was only the sound of his breathing, slow and even. She fancied she felt it caress her cheek, but it was a ridiculous thought to savor now when her world had been pulled out from under her.

"Who's the groom?" The muscle in his jaw tightened and he clenched his hands almost possessively at her waist.

"Monsieur Beaudin," she whispered.

"He doesn't deserve you." The words were so emphatic and blasphemous, spoken there in the hallway just outside her uncle's door, that they shocked her. Did he know? Did he have any idea that she was a prisoner in every sense of the word?

She searched his face, looking for the meaning behind them, but the momentary ferocity brought about with those words had gone and his handsome face was impassive again. Still, she couldn't stop the flush of pleasure they evoked as she settled on his eyes. They were dark like the clouds of a thunderstorm. She'd never seen anything like them.

"Who would deserve me?" She hadn't meant to ask, but his intense stare had hypnotized the question from her.

That stare never wavered when he answered. "Somebody who'll take care of you."

His words were so pleasing she closed her eyes briefly to revel in them. She'd almost forgotten what it meant to be taken care of, to not wake up every morning and battle the fear that constantly plagued her. Life with Anton would be a gross continuation of her life with Jean. Never knowing when she might displease him. Never knowing when a remark might provoke him to strike her or give her a week locked away in her room with scarcely enough food to sustain her. She'd learned to gauge Jean so those things rarely happened now, but with Anton she'd have to start over.

But Gray... She took in a long, shuddering breath. Gray was a protector. The woman who was lucky enough to be his would never know fear. There would be so much more. It was those thoughts of more that made her become aware of the impropriety of their near-embrace and slowly push herself away from him. His hands dropped from her waist with a lingering caress that she imagined was intentional, while her own hands reluctantly returned to her sides.

"I'm afraid the question of my care doesn't figure into things." She attempted a parting smile. "Thank you." And she started to walk past him, but his eyes held hers a little longer. There was something deep and longing there, but impossible to explore. So she walked to the stairs while trying to pretend that she couldn't still feel his hands on her, that she wouldn't perpetually relive that brief moment in his arms. It was the only time he had touched her, and she knew she'd never forget it.

Chapter Two

Gray took a long, final drag from his cigarillo before flicking it and sending it flying in a high arc into the street. The orange glow of the tip bounced twice before settling in the dirt to slowly burn out. He wanted his hunger for Sophie to burn out just as easily, but it wouldn't. No matter how he tried, he couldn't forget the hopelessness on her face that morning. He wanted to think of her as he thought of Jean LaSalle: cold, remote, arrogant. But she wasn't any of those. She tried to be stoic but her eyes gave her away; he wanted to know what they hid from the world.

Watching her walk away from him had been harder than it should have been. Even now he could recall the faint trace of honeysuckle she had left behind and how he had stood there breathing it in until her scent too had gone. The warmth of her body still clung to his hands where he'd held her.

He wanted to forget, but his eyes kept drifting to her anyway. Through the floor-to-ceiling windows of the Nelsons' mansion, they found her effortlessly among the other dancers. With her crown of golden hair and deep blue gown she could have been one of the angels on LaSalle's ceiling. His gaze drifted down to the way the gown clung to her small waist and then the creamy globes of flesh that threatened to spill from its bodice. No, he amended, she was too earthy to be angelic. He forced his gaze from that temptation to her face. She was smiling, but it was strained and didn't meet her eyes. They were turbulent like the pale, clear blue of a mountain stream in spring.

She was dancing with Anton Beaudin. The lustful gleam in the man's eye was unmistakable and it immediately made Gray angry, though he was her intended groom and had every right to his thoughts. But the idea of Sophie giving herself to that cocky bastard made Gray want to smash his fist into the man's face. His jaw tensed as he turned away from the window.

A vision of her in his own arms flashed through his mind, and he immediately checked the unwarranted thought. There were many reasons she couldn't be his. Not the least of which was that she was the niece of his enemy. The fact that LaSalle was the meanest son of a bitch he'd ever come across was further deterrent.

He tried to remind himself that this was simply a bad case of lust. The obvious cure for which would be to spend a night—or several—in Victoria House, the elegant gaming hall and brothel across town. He could probably even find a woman who looked like Sophie if the lights were turned down. The problem was that he'd still have to see her until the job was done. He'd still have to stand by quietly as she suffered. He'd have to smell her honeysuckle scent and endure the kindness in her eyes every single time she walked past him.

He'd be reminded every single day that it was more than lust he felt for her. She awoke something inside him that he couldn't easily silence.

Gray shook his head and reminded himself he had a job to do. Sophie Buchanan was nothing but a distraction and she'd probably hate him when his task was finished. The sooner she got married the better.

He forced his gaze to the street, taking in every shadow and examining it for a threat. Looking for danger was a habit to him by now. Something he did automatically. LaSalle was a son of a bitch with many enemies and they were liable to be lurking anywhere.

The scuff of boot tread on wood caught his attention a moment before Hunter Jameson appeared from the other end of the wraparound porch. The Jamesons were LaSalle's main rival in the copper industry in this part of Montana Territory. In fact, rumors had been flying that LaSalle would arrange a marriage for his niece with Hunter in a gesture that would join the two empires. Anyone who thought that, however, didn't know how greedy LaSalle was by nature. He wasn't about to share his wealth.

Though Hunter's father was almost as suspect as LaSalle, Gray had found Hunter to be likable. They had met once when Gray had intervened with a runaway horse and saved the man from being run down. Now they were cordial when they met at events around town, usually when Gray was working as escort for LaSalle.

"Evening, Gray."

"Hunter."

"I was hoping I'd see you here tonight. I'm heading out in the morning and hoped you'd reconsidered the job offer."

Hunter had offered him a job on the spot when Gray had saved his life. "I can't."

Hunter shook his head. "That's too bad."

"Monsieur Sinclair, please, if someone could just take me home."

Sophie's voice with its soft French intonations carried to him. It wasn't a heavily accented voice like LaSalle's. The inflection could only be heard in the occasional word, just often enough to make him listen for it. Everything inside him stopped at the sound of her distress. He glanced over to make sure she was okay. She stood outside the closed terrace doors with her cape around her shoulders.

Hunter cleared his throat, drawing Gray's attention back to

him. The man grinned and rubbed a hand over his jaw. "I think I understand."

Shit. He had to do better so his attraction to her wasn't as noticeable.

"I've already committed to finishing this job," Gray said.

"Send word to me if you change your mind." Hunter tipped his head and hurried down the steps.

"Safe travel," Gray called after him.

Then he went back to scanning the street, visibly as vigilant as he was supposed to be, but ravenously drinking up the sound of her voice as she pleaded with Sinclair again.

Sinclair, who was in charge of security, stood before her, his back slightly blocking her, so that Gray had to move closer to hear the conversation.

"It's almost midnight. Supper will be served soon. Don't you think eating something will make you feel better?" Sinclair was saying.

"I just need to go home...please."

There was a moment of silence and then. "I'll need to check with your uncle."

"Go to LaSalle. I'll take her." Gray heard himself offer. Sinclair was usually the one assigned to Sophie's needs but, as the most trusted gunslinger, he had been ordered to attend a midnight meeting LaSalle had planned later that night with some important men in town for the ball.

Sinclair looked over at him, a glimmer of relief on his face, and gave a nod of thanks. "She'll be okay with Brand at the house.""

"I'll be quick." Gray assured him.

"You remember the safe combination for the jewels?"

"Yes, I have everything under control," Gray said.

"Good."

Gray left to get the buggy, berating himself for volunteering. He was supposed to keep his distance. Anyone else could have been dispatched to see her home. But there was no reason it shouldn't be Gray. No one knew how badly he wanted her. No one knew that he dreamed at night of taking her over his horse and fleeing with her across the plains where no one would find them. No one knew how very little was stopping him from doing just that.

Chapter Three

Sophie felt a twinge of longing twist deep within her as she watched Gray approach. In the darkness his eyes held a dangerous glint that made him look more forbidding than usual. His hair hung loose past his shoulders. She wanted to have one conversation with him unhindered by all that stood between them. Would he be as kind to her as his eyes sometimes suggested?

"Miss Buchanan." Those eyes settled on her as he extended his hand to help her down the steps of the Nelsons' house. None of his earlier compassion was reflected there. The gray was flat and closed off.

Sophie looked down to see his palm outstretched to her and her mouth went dry. That brief moment in the hall was the first time they'd touched at all. Now she was about to touch him again. If only she wasn't wearing gloves. Her fingertips tingled before they slipped across his rough palm and his fingers closed around them. His hand was warm and strong, completely engulfing hers. A current almost like electricity traveled the length of her arm. She glanced up to see if he felt the connection, too, but he was already looking toward the buggy, away from her, as he helped her down the steps. She felt a bizarre desire to prolong the contact, but in seconds she was seated in the waiting buggy and there was no reason to not let go. So she did.

His touch was nothing like Monsieur Beaudin's, or Anton, as he insisted she call him now. Anton, with his cold, possessive hand almost constantly at her waist, failed to stir any feeling at all within her except maybe disgust. While Gray, without even trying, stirred far too many feelings. It was a dangerous attraction. She knew that, *had* known it from the first time she saw him, but it hadn't stopped her from thinking about him. Maybe it was the wedding looming before her making her bolder, but she knew an undeniable longing to discover if the attraction was mutual.

"We meet again today, Monsieur Gray."

When he merely took up the reins and clicked a command for the horse to start, she glanced over at him.

"Thank you for taking me home. I'm already feeling much better."

He gave a curt nod. "Did something happen inside?"

"No, nothing out of the ordinary. I'm tired."

The only difference was that she couldn't bear the way Anton looked at her now. Like he owned her. But she was loath to bring up Anton. His name had no place between them.

They rode onward in silence. She sighed and bemoaned her lack of experience in flirtation. If Gray did find her attractive, he certainly hid it well. She'd thought that moment in the hall meant that maybe he did. But what had she expected? No man looked at her as anything other than LaSalle property. She never even danced with anyone except Jean or Anton and the occasional business associate approved by her uncle. Her only chaperones were the gunslingers in Jean's inner circle. Who would dare threaten her virtue?

"Do you want to marry him?"

The question was asked so softly, Sophie wondered if she had heard him correctly. A small fluttering of nerves began deep in her belly. She wanted to be honest, to rekindle that spark of closeness from the hallway, but she had learned to not trust easily. Everyone she knew reported back to Jean. How did she know if Gray would be any different?

As far as she knew, he hadn't mentioned to her uncle what happened this morning. Still. She hedged. "I do want children. I've always seen myself married."

"But to Beaudin?"

She closed her eyes, intending to conjure an image of the hated man, but instead she saw Gray holding her in an embrace that only a husband should. "I don't know."

But she did know.

They turned onto Last Ditch Gulch and meandered slowly along the main street. Gray's expression was in shadow but the occasional streetlamp allowed her to ascertain that he was thoughtful. They rode in silence, the only sounds the steady clip-clop of the horse and the occasional drunken laughter in the distance. Two-story shops loomed dark on either side of them. She watched him from her peripheral vision, taking in the gun holstered at his side and the leather thong that tied it to his thigh. The mark of his profession.

"I meant what I said earlier." he said. "You deserve a man, not that snake."

The words were almost angry and inexplicably made her smile. Maybe the chemistry she thought she'd imagined had been real. He was attracted to her. The knowledge gave her senses permission to acknowledge his closeness. She could *feel* him at her side even though over a dozen inches separated them. That space between them became charged with his energy. It rippled along the length of her thigh and up her side.

"You seem very much a man, Monsieur Gray." The thought escaped before she had a chance to hold it back.

She heard his quick, indrawn breath and closed her eyes. Sometimes her recklessness ran away with her. "Sometimes I say outrageous things when I'm nervous."

"Why are you nervous?" His gaze pinned her, making the

fluttering in her belly begin in earnest.

"I-I don't know." The question held a dangerous undertone and she wasn't entirely sure she should encourage it.

His gaze touched her face before turning back to the road. When he did, she let out a breath she hadn't even been aware of holding. Maybe it was best to leave things unspoken.

No. She had wanted this time with him and she'd gotten it. Who knew if she would have this chance again?

"You make me nervous because I...I like you."

He took in a breath. "You like me?"

"Yes, and I hope you like me."

Like. Such a poor word choice. It implied so much while saying nothing. She liked Monsieur Sinclair because he taught her how to play billiards and cards during the long winter months. He was a friend, sort of. Friendship with men in her uncle's employ was always precarious. Their loyalty was to him and not her.

Her feelings for Gray were much more visceral and romantic. Sitting next to him made her feel like she had champagne in her veins and the bubbles were effervescing through her.

They turned left onto the street that would take them home. Their time together was almost over. She gripped the cool metal bar that edged the back of the seat as she turned to him.

"Do you?" she asked.

"Like you?" He refused to look at her. His gaze was focused on the road ahead and his hands tightened on the reins, as if they were on a treacherous mountain pass and the horses hadn't navigated this street a thousand times.

She couldn't help but smile. It felt like they were school children, neither of them willing to admit their feelings first.

"Or perhaps you think I'm spoiled. Sometimes people do. They see how much money Jean has and think I must be a pampered princess."

This made him glance at her with a raised brow. Now that they weren't on the main road the lights weren't around to reveal him to her, his entire face was in shadow. A boon and a curse. It made her more rash, but she missed the nuance of his expression.

"I don't think you're spoiled," he said and turned his attention back to the road.

Well, that was something. She sat back, willing herself to be content with that much.

"I think you're kind...and beautiful."

His voice was soft so as not to carry on the wind, but deep and true. Her cheeks burned with pleasure and she smiled.

He thought she was kind and beautiful.

They drove the remaining three blocks in silence before pulling to a stop in front of the imposing three-story brick and stone mansion. She tried not to notice the warmth of his hand this time as he helped her down, but he practically singed her through her gloves.

He walked slightly behind her as they ascended the front

steps, his quiet strength making her heart pound. She loved how he towered over her.

Monsieur Brand met them on the porch. "You're home early, Miss Buchanan."

His brows drew together in puzzlement as he hurried to open the front door for them.

"I wasn't feeling well. Monsieur Gray offered to drive me home since Mr. Sinclair was occupied."

"Ah, well, I hope you feel better soon," he said. To Gray, he added, "I'll wait for you here."

Sophie smiled to herself. Usually, Monsieur Sinclair followed her to her room to collect her jewels and return them to the safe. Monsieur Brand was his second in charge, so she had half expected him to accompany her upstairs.

She kept silent as she walked inside and then up the elegantly curved mahogany staircase. Gray followed. The muffled sound of his boots on the stairs reverberated through her. But it was the prickling of the skin along her back that told her how close he was. Something delicious and wicked flickered to life within her and settled low, just below her stomach.

She'd never felt excitement like it before and it made her hesitate a moment at her bedroom door. She should tell him to wait in the hallway, but as soon as she had the thought, she knew she wouldn't. Taking a deep breath, she opened the door to see Anne, her maid, jump up in surprise. Whether it was alarm at Sophie's early arrival or consternation at the tall figure that followed her inside, she didn't know.

"Thank you, Anne." Sophie tugged off her gloves and placed them on the small table by the door. "I can manage tonight. Go to bed." She heard the words coming from her mouth but had no idea why she was dismissing the only person who might help her keep a grip on the sanity she felt slipping away. Because she wanted to be alone with Gray, and that was something that should not happen.

Chapter Four

The maid hesitated awkwardly, her gaze going from Sophie to Gray and back again, before she gave a brief curtsy and left. Sophie opened her mouth to apologize for her maid and explain she was new but realized he would know that. Jean only allowed her to keep a maid for about six months before finding some reason to dismiss her or move her to other duties. Yet another way that he kept Sophie isolated.

Gray didn't seem to notice, though, as he stepped into her room and stood looking around. The furniture was dainty with swirls in the wood and gilded etchings. It was silly, but it seemed so intimate to have this rugged man in her private sanctum. The only place that was hers. His very presence had her blushing.

When his gaze settled on the blue satin counterpane across

the bed, she quickly moved to her dressing table across the room. Having him here made her heart pound too fast. He should go. She placed her sapphire earbobs on the polished surface and reached for the clasp of her necklace, but her fingers trembled too badly to get it open.

"Let me help." Gray's voice moved over her like rough velvet, causing her intimate muscles to tighten curiously.

Sophie's wide-eyed gaze met his in the mirror as he came up behind her. A full head and neck taller than her petite frame, his deep stare held hers briefly before he looked down to the clasp. Sophie barely had time to recover from the intensity of that look before his fingertips touched the sensitive flesh of her nape. The contact sent thrills of excitement through her and made her clench her teeth to keep from visibly reacting.

The clasp opened and the long, heavy strand of sapphires and diamonds tugged across her neck and shoulder in a slow caress as it came away in his hands. It landed softly on the dresser and then his hand was on her shoulder. Her shocked gaze came up to find his in the mirror, but it wasn't there. He was watching his hand move slowly down the smooth skin of her arm. She looked, too, and became immediately fascinated by the contrast of his large hand against her pale skin. She watched its leisurely progress until it covered her own hand, leaving her flesh tingling in its wake.

Sophie wasn't sure who initiated the movement, but suddenly she found her back pressed lightly against the solid strength of his chest. His other arm crossed over in front of her and she realized she was in the loose cage of his embrace, where she wanted to be. She watched his graceful fingers as they efficiently divested her of her bracelet and placed it with the necklace on the dressing table.

His body tensed as if to move, and she realized how badly she wanted him to stay. Nothing could happen, but she didn't want the moment to end.

"My hairpins, too. They're made of diamonds."

Her gaze flicked to his in the mirror and she saw something there, something hot and smoldering. She welcomed its implication. Gray inhaled deeply as his hands released her wrist and moved to her hair. Sophie closed her eyes and savored his touch as one by one the pins dropped to the polished surface with a click. Her hair fell around her shoulders and he might have stroked it once. The movement was so butterfly soft she couldn't be sure, but the sensation reverberated within her a hundred times over.

If only things were different.

The sixth and last pin dropped and Sophie reluctantly forced herself back to earth. But when she turned to thank him for his help, Gray's hands rested heavily on the dressing table on either side of her and he didn't step back. She looked up but her gaze never made it past his perfect bow lips. She wanted to kiss them. To just once feel them on hers.

In her room, shielded from the rest of the world by the

breadth of his body, it seemed like one kiss was possible. Just one before everything changed and she was forced to go to Anton. Didn't she deserve just one moment of joy?

Before she could stop herself, Sophie leaned up on her tiptoes and pressed her lips to his. They were warm and firm as they parted in shock beneath her. His breath washed over her. He was going to pull away. She could feel him gathering himself to do just that.

She made a soft sound of protest in the back of her throat. A sound she didn't recognize, and it made him pause. His lips softened and parted over hers, moving gently and coaxing more from her. Then she tried something she had no idea she knew how to do; she touched his perfect bottom lip with the tip of her tongue.

Gray groaned softly. She fairly purred at the sound and her palms moved up his arms to his shoulders. His hands closed on her hips and pulled her against him causing her to gasp at the contact of her front to his. He pressed the advantage and the tip of his tongue gently pushed inside to brush hers. The foreign sensation of him, hot and moist in her mouth, made her blood thicken and pool deep in that newly awakened part of her. He must have known, because his hands moved down below the bustle of her dress to cup her bottom where it met her thighs and pull her tight against him. Something hard pressed against her stomach.

It should have frightened her; she thought she knew what it

was, but nothing about Gray, aside from the intensity of her feelings for him, frightened her. She didn't want an inch of space between them, so her arms circled his shoulders and she pulled herself closer. His fingers tightened as a low and primitive sound came from his throat. And suddenly the kiss became something she never expected. It became the conversation that always existed, hovering between them but never expressed in words.

It was hungry and unrestrained and so much more intimate than she had ever thought a kiss could be. And, all too soon, even that wasn't enough. Gray moved her back until she felt the press of the table against her thighs and she knew what he wanted. Closer. Her hands blindly pushed the jewelry to the side, and he lifted her so she sat on the edge, her thighs pushed apart so that he could settle between them.

He kissed her again before his fingers tangled in her hair to pull her head back. She was reluctant to lose his mouth until it began blazing a path of open-mouthed kisses down her neck. Then he settled on the swells of her breasts and breathed in deeply, inhaling her scent.

"Gray," she whispered and curled her fingers around the warmth of his neck. If this was all they could have then she wanted it all. She wanted as much from this stolen moment as they could possibly squeeze. "Yes."

It was all the encouragement he needed. He tugged on the silk of her bodice and the cool night air touched a breast, only to be replaced by the wet heat of his mouth. Sophie gasped and held him to her as odd pulses of pleasure shot to her groin when he suckled her. She gave herself up to the decadence of his mouth feasting on her and dropped her head back against the cool mirror, eyes heavy-lidded with passion. It probably would have taken her a lot longer to notice it, except he paused and pulled back enough to drink in the sight of her exposed to him. The pause made her open her eyes and that's when she saw the door behind him.

It was still open.

His mouth settled on her again and suddenly she realized the picture they would present if someone should happen by. A small part of her wondered if the pleasure might be worth the inevitable punishment, but no. There was no telling what Jean would do to Gray.

"Gray." It was a whisper, too soft to dispel his passion. Then more urgently. "Gray! The door is open. Mon Dieu, the door!"

Shit!

Gray pushed away from Sophie with such force he propelled himself backward several feet and made the dressing table wobble precariously. What the hell had happened to him? He'd only meant to help her with her jewelry but her warmth, her scent, the sweet innocence in her eyes had been his undoing. And when she'd pressed her lips to his, he'd told himself one kiss wouldn't hurt anything. He'd never meant for it to go further, never meant to put his mouth on her body. If anyone had seen them—he didn't even want to think of that. Even now, chest heaving from lack of air and an excess of adrenaline, he couldn't tear his eyes from the sight of her nipple, pink and glistening from his attention.

Thankfully, she became aware because she had the good grace to blush and pull up her gown. Then, more slowly, she pushed forward until she dropped down to stand on the thick carpet. Gray would have helped her but his hands shook and he wasn't entirely sure what he would do if he touched her again.

"Why did you do that?" His voice was harsher than he intended.

She bit her bottom lip, clearly as confused as he was. "I...I'm sorry. I wanted to kiss you. I've wanted to kiss you for a long time."

Gray might have laughed. Even he wasn't sure what the harsh exhalation of air meant. She surprised him. But it wasn't a subject he was willing to discuss. She was off limits and the sooner he put distance between them the better. The longer he stayed in her room, the more his good sense deserted him.

"Is that all the jewelry?" He took a step toward the pile on the dresser but waited for her to move out of the way before he approached it, still unable to trust himself with her.

"Yes."

Gray picked up the sapphires and diamonds and suddenly hated himself for having to take them away from her. He paused and looked at the pile in his hands. They must be worth a small fortune. Then he noticed her dressing table held only a few bottles of perfume, a pot of skin cream, and assorted cosmetics. It was devoid of the jewelry box he expected.

"He doesn't let you keep any jewelry at all, does he?"

Gray had followed her to her room because Sinclair had mentioned the safe. Usually, Sinclair followed her upstairs and waited for the maid to hand the jewelry over to him, so that he could put it in the safe in LaSalle's study. Gray had convinced himself that the jewelry was important in some way, family heirlooms. He had not expected her to not have any jewelry at all in her room.

When she didn't answer he pinned her with his gaze. "No," she whispered.

"Why?"

No answer.

But she didn't need to answer. LaSalle wanted to keep her. To keep her he had to make certain she had no means of running away.

"You don't want to marry that bastard, do you?"

She reluctantly shook her head and there was a suspicious sheen in her eyes.

Gray noticed it and detested the twin spasms of pain and anger that shot through his heart. "Dammit!"

He didn't want to care. He didn't want to want her. He left her there before he could descend any further into madness.

Chapter Five

Gray had broken the only rule Sinclair had given him. He had become personally involved. This was supposed to be a job like any other. Protect the target until it was time to bring him down. LaSalle was the target. His niece wasn't supposed to figure into things. She was someone in LaSalle's sphere, so she was someone they had to protect, but she wasn't important to their mission.

Gray wasn't supposed to touch her. Kiss her. Begin to lose his heart to her. Two weeks had passed since he'd blasted through that boundary and he could still feel her in his hands, taste her on his lips.

"You seem agitated. Everything all right?"

Gray hadn't realized he was staring into the window of the

dress shop until Sinclair's voice interrupted the downward spiral of his thoughts. Sophie was in there for another fitting for her wedding gown where she had been all evening. She usually went after hours, when Martine could focus on her alone. The shopkeeper was her friend, so he assumed much of that time was spent lamenting her upcoming wedding in the privacy of the shop.

"I'm fine." Gray turned toward the street where he should have been facing the entire time. Any threat would come from that direction, not inside.

Sinclair didn't seem convinced. He glanced through the window, but he wouldn't see anything. The women had already disappeared into the back room.

"We haven't had a chance to talk much since we learned of the wedding." He stepped close and kept his voice low as his gaze took in the shadows around them. "I've heard back and it's confirmed. Everything will come together at the wedding."

They had discussed this plan before. All of LaSalle's associates and even some enemies would be in attendance. It would be the perfect time to get them all together and arrest them at once. It made sense, but Gray didn't like it.

"You're sure they're coming?" he asked.

Sinclair nodded. "I saw Miss Buchanan updating the guest list myself, and later I looked at the responses she received. Every last one of them is planning to attend."

Finally, they would all face justice. LaSalle had spent the last several years building his empire. He was attempting to buy up all of the land with mining potential, whether people wanted to sell to him or not. If they refused, he'd use force or coercion to make them. Sometimes people went missing or were found dead. He never got his own hands dirty, which is why it was taking so long to bring him to justice. He used a couple of different companies and hired men, including his good friend Beaudin, to handle the negotiations.

Sinclair, a deputy marshal, had been working to get him for a couple years already and finally had evidence of all involved. The problem facing Sinclair the past couple months was getting them all in one place. For a while, it looked like they would have to take the chance and arrest them separately. The big issue with that was coordinating the operation so they were all arrested at the same time. Even the difference of a couple hours would leave it to chance that someone would find out and go on the run. The wedding was the perfect opportunity to get them all together in one place, which eliminated that problem.

"I still don't like it." Gray had voiced his concern with this plan when they first conceived of it. "It puts Miss Buchanan in danger."

"She's always been in danger. Comes with being related to LaSalle," Sinclair said.

"What of the other guests? Any one of them could get hurt." Gray was grasping at straws and he knew it.

"I agree, it's not ideal, but we don't have a choice. We have to end this now, and we have to arrest more than LaSalle and Beaudin. I have extra men coming in to help. If all goes to plan, we'll be able to take them before the wedding even starts."

Gray knew he was right, but he didn't like it. Even without the danger, it could all go so wrong that Sophie would still end up married to Beaudin. If a couple of the guests didn't show, they would have to regroup and try another time, which meant the wedding would go forward as scheduled and she would be married to that ass.

This is why he should have kept his hands off her. She compromised his judgement. His loyalty in this should be bringing LaSalle to justice. Not keeping her from marrying Beaudin.

"She doesn't want to marry him," he said anyway.

Sinclair took in a meaningful breath and Gray braced himself for the inevitable question. He wouldn't lie about his feelings for her.

"Gray...have you...?" His voice trailed off as Gray came to attention.

"Look," Gray said, his eyes following the single figure in black that crossed the road a couple of blocks down.

The woman wore widow's weeds, a black dress and a hat with a veil. She might have been anyone, but something about her called to him. It was in the unique grace she used in holding her skirts up so they wouldn't drag the ground; such a common, feminine movement, but he recognized it somehow. He had spent so much time over the past several months watching Sophie that he knew how she walked and moved around the world. She led with her left hand, even though someone must have taught her along the way that she must use her right because that's the hand she used to write, in everything else she favored her left hand. That's the hand she used to grab the railing as she hurried up the steps across the street.

"It's Miss Buchanan. Go inside to the dressmaker. I'll follow her."

"You're sure it's her?" Sinclair asked, glancing inside the window to make sure she wasn't in there.

"It's her." The rhythm of her step, the sway of her hips, the set of her shoulders; they were minor things, but Gray could have picked them out given a thousand women to choose from. "She's escaping."

He'd been waiting for this ever since she'd admitted she didn't want the marriage. That desperate sadness in her eyes had led him to believe she would try something.

"Damn," Sinclair muttered.

When Gray went to hurry down the steps, Sinclair stopped him with a hand on his arm. "Wait. Beaudin's men."

Beaudin had had men on her ever since the marriage had been arranged. Two of them were watching now from across the road. Gray had nearly forgotten them. He wasn't thinking clearly which was dangerous.

"If they suspect a thing, Beaudin might demand to move up the wedding," Sinclair said very reasonably. "We can't let them know she's trying to escape."

Gray was in full agreement with that, though likely for different reasons. He didn't want the bastard to get his hands on Sophie. "I'll follow her." She was farther down the block now, almost completely lost to the gray of twilight. He had to hurry. "I'll take her to my room. You take Miss Martine home in her place. We'll meet back here tomorrow morning and switch them."

"They'll never know," Sinclair agreed. The men had been swilling from a bottle of whiskey ever since they'd gotten here. "I'll send the carriage around to the back door and sneak the dressmaker in. Go."

Gray didn't need further prompting. Aware of Beaudin's men watching him, he sauntered across the road in the direction of the saloon until they lost interest, probably having assumed he was off duty for the night. The very moment they stopped watching, he hurried down an alley and in Sophie's direction, determined to find her again.

Chapter Six

A politician or corporate figure had graced their table almost every night since Sophie had been informed of her wedding. She was forced to play hostess while Jean bribed his way to lower taxes or cheaper timber. Everything was a game with him as he looked for ways to turn his copper into gold. She had no choice but to don the facade she had become so adept at wearing and be a pretty fixture at the table.

It was a facade that had taken her many years and many punishments to cultivate. She'd been ten when her parents had died in the mine explosion. It had been a Sunday and Jean had invited them to go see the progress being made. No one was supposed to be working. But the dynamite had exploded anyway, leaving Jean unscathed. Three years passed before it even occurred to her that he might have had a hand in the accident. She only thought it then because she'd overheard him arguing with Alexandre, who was fifteen by then and too hotheaded to keep his opinions to himself.

The memory of how badly her brother had been beaten still caused her to shudder. She'd begged him to leave and so he had, with a promise to come back for her. But ever since then she'd had trouble hiding her own suspicions and continuing to be the biddable niece. Her resentment was clear in every word, every action, and it hadn't taken long for Jean to grow weary of it. She'd felt the wrath of his cane across her legs and back more times than she cared to remember.

Finally, she'd learned to control those rebellious impulses. As long as she played the role he wanted, nothing bad happened. Occasionally she'd still push too far and be struck for it or locked in her room, but nothing like before. It was livable. But with Anton she'd have to learn all over again. And what would be demanded of her would be so much more than she could give.

So while Jean had schemed over those dinners, Sophie had quietly plotted her escape. She refused to live like this any longer. He had left on a trip to visit a mine this morning, and the perfect opportunity had presented itself. Escape was the only way to save herself. She planned to run to her brother in Chicago, but first she needed funds.

This was how Sophie found herself awkwardly arched over a green felt-topped billiard table in the back of Victoria House attempting to sink the last of her balls into the corner pocket. The gaming hell was the only place that might be safe enough for what she had planned. The saloons in town were known to be rough. Victoria House was run by a woman, Glory Winters, and it was rumored that she welcomed women in her establishment. She even provided protection in the form of doormen who kept a watchful eye over the crowd. It was the first place Sophie thought to go.

A bead of nervous sweat rolled down her back causing an itch between her shoulder blades that was destined to go unattended to. For the first time that night her scheme seemed like a bad idea. The mood of the crowd that had gathered to watch the spectacle had gone from revelry after the first game she had won to something darker.

For the life of her, Sophie did not understand exactly what had precipitated the change. But her fingers twitched around her cue stick in awareness, and she straightened, pretending to assess the shot from a different angle. The hum of conversation resumed somewhat.

The crowd had moved too close, forcing her to brush against them on her way around the table to take the shot from the other side. The wall on that side was much too close to afford many unhampered shots but she sought the sanctuary it offered more than anything else. Just on her way around the last corner, a large hand shot out from the crush and fitted itself to her hip. She was too shocked to protest and then a low voice behind her said, "Throw the shot."

Gray! It was unmistakably his voice. He hadn't spoken to her directly since the night of their kiss, but she recognized it.

She froze. Then she frowned because it meant they—her uncle's gunslingers—knew she was here and if they did, so would her uncle. And she had planned her escape so carefully. Despair held a death grip on her lungs, but she refused to give into it. She might have been found but she hadn't been captured yet. Her gaze flicked to the two piles of cash resting under a heavy marker on the table's bank at the other end. Her contribution had been desperately hidden away one dollar at a time over the years.

It represented freedom and it was hers if she sank the shot.

She moved to continue, ignoring Gray, but his hand moved to her wrist in a grip that refused to be ignored. "We'll never make it out of here if you don't."

That made her look over her shoulder at him. Gray wasn't looking at her but at the other end of the table. He merely nodded toward to the group situated behind the cash. Jeb, the man she was competing against, stood there in deep discussion with a few rather unfriendly looking characters. Those men had not been there earlier. Not when she'd beaten Jeb in the first game ten minutes ago and certainly not when he had so graciously proposed a double or nothing scenario.

Jeb looked back at her, a deep scowl darkening his features, and her heart sank. He was angry. And then the group around him looked at her and she actually blanched. Something menacing gleamed deep in their eyes.

"The lady forfeits." Gray's voice carried loud and strong across the table and over the din of the crowd.

Sophie immediately took exception to his interference and opened her mouth to say so but then closed it, mentally evaluating the possible outcomes. If she sank the shot, would she be allowed to walk away unscathed? The looks the men gave her suggested not.

"Does she know that?" Jeb laughed, a hollow sound without mirth. He pushed his greasy hair back from a brow that was prematurely creased from years in the sun. She had pegged him for a ranch hand, but outlaws also spent a lot of time outdoors.

Gray came around her then and she found herself pushed behind his shoulder. The movement was so abrupt that the veil of her hat came tumbling down over her face. She had borrowed the whole ensemble from Martine as a means of escaping from the dress shop undetected. She pushed up the stiff lace so she could see.

"Doesn't matter. She forfeits," Gray said.

Sophie was grudgingly beginning to accept that Gray's assistance was needed to get her out of the situation, but hearing herself relegated to an insignificant detail was more than she could take.

"Now—" She started to interject but his hand pressed lightly against her stomach and halted anything she might have said.

"Just who are you?" Jeb persisted.

Gray pushed the drape of his coat back. The men as a group looked down towards his hip where he undoubtedly kept his gun holstered. Guns weren't allowed in the establishment, another reason she had chosen it. How had he gotten it inside? She glanced toward the room's entrance to see if the doorman had noticed, but everyone outside of their bubble seemed oblivious to what was happening.

One of the men muttered something to the others. It was too low for her to hear but created a rumble in the folks gathered round. Surely they must have noticed he was something of a professional.

"You her husband?" Jeb asked. It was a peace offering and when she heard it Sophie grasped Gray's forearm where it still rested against her.

Gray's head lowered slightly in a move that could have been considered affirmation if the receiver was so inclined.

"Well, I accept her forfeit," the man said. "But on the condition that you tan her arse when you get her home. A lady," he snickered when he said the word as if that did not describe her in the least, "should know to mind her menfolk."

Sophie cringed with anger. Was it her fault he was a sore loser? Was it her fault he had assumed she didn't know how to play? Well, maybe she *had* played up that part a bit.

Without responding to the man, Gray grabbed her elbow and began to steer them away from the table. Sophie's gaze fell on the cash and she realized it was more than she could walk away from. "Wait! I want my money back." She could accept forfeiting her winnings, but she should at least walk away with the amount she had brought to the table.

"Sophie!" Gray breathed angrily near her ear, while staying focused on the men and the potential danger.

Jeb was already busy thumbing through the bills, but he heard her. "Get that bitch out of here."

She didn't see Gray move but the next sound she heard was the resonant gasp of the crowd as they stared at him, his gun poised to be released from its holster.

"Just the lady's portion." Gray offered reasonably. "Else..." He let the word hang in the air, allowing the men to decide if the amount was worth the bullet at least one of them would sport otherwise.

Jeb seriously seemed to consider the alternative. After all, he wasn't holding a gun. Chances were good he would avoid a bullet in the first round. But then he pulled out some bills and slid them across the table.

Gray smoothly leaned over and collected them, pushing them into his pocket and backing away at the same time.

"Gray?" An authoritative voice, rich and masculine, cut through the thick silence of the room. A large, well-dressed man walked into the room as if he'd just been summoned, his attention focused on what was happening.

"Able." Gray greeted him without looking away from Jeb and

his friends. "We're on our way out."

Able's discerning glare shifted to Jeb and his friends. "I'll make sure they don't follow you."

"I appreciate your help," Gray said and slid his gun back into its holster.

Sophie turned and led the way through the crowd that politely parted for them, not daring to stop until they had reached the street. Even then, Gray held onto her arm until they were well away from the establishment.

"Let me go. You don't have to pull me along like a child." She snapped and jerked her arm away. She hadn't decided if she should be more grateful to him or angry for his interference. Both were valid.

"Put down your veil."

She complied but it hardly seemed necessary given the fact that the people she had hoped to avoid, Gray and his cohorts, had found her.

"Beaudin." He supplied in answer to her unvoiced question. "He has men watching."

Sophie gasped and looked around. The street was fairly crowded with evening pedestrians but no one seemed to be following them. The very idea that Anton felt he had the right to monitor her movements made her furious.

"Do you think anyone recognized me?" It seemed far-fetched considering not many people knew her since her uncle kept her isolated. The few people she knew from his business dealings and Society events hadn't been at the gaming hall. "How did you know that man? Able?"

"I don't think anyone recognized you. I worked there for a time, that's how he knew me and why they didn't check me for a gun when I walked in."

Well, that answered her next question.

He kept looking around as if expecting a threat to pop out of the shadows. In fact, he was walking so fast she had to almost run to keep up.

No one seemed to notice them, though, or if they thought it odd that a man dressed in buckskin trousers and duster would be escorting a finely dressed woman like her in this part of town, they kept it to themselves. She had borrowed a stiff and somber black gown from Martine, but the modiste didn't do subtle well. The skirt was striped with thin panels of dark gray satin and accompanied by a smart, hip-length jacket that accentuated the narrow waist of its wearer.

It was a moment more before she calmed down enough to realize Gray wasn't leading her back to the dress shop or even home. They were going farther into the rougher part of town, marked by the uneven boardwalk beneath her feet and then the complete lack of one at all. The buildings here were all of wood and badly weathered.

"Where are we going?" There was only a faint tremor to her voice, but she halted abruptly.

It took a couple of steps for Gray to realize she had stopped, and when he did, he was smiling as he walked back to her. A wicked smile that caused a shiver of foreboding to travel up her spine. "Too late for that. You should've thought of the consequences before running away."

With that, he grabbed her arm in a firm grip and pulled her around a corner where he urged her up a rickety flight of stairs affixed to the side of a mercantile store. At the top he stopped to unlock the single door before pushing her into the dark room beyond.

Chapter Seven

The door closed behind her and the key turned in the lock with a click of finality. For one tense second, Sophie wasn't sure if he had locked her in alone or if he was here with her. But she could feel him behind her. His presence as strong and steady here as it had always been back home.

She took a deep breath to calm herself and was enveloped by the soothing embrace of his scent. Why she would find his scent soothing or even recognize it so readily left her shaking her head. It was completely illogical and really very presumptuous, but the tension that had made her shoulders so tight since she'd left Martine's began to ease. She wasn't afraid.

This was his home. It smelled of leather and something else. Probably his cigarillos. Not the pungent, heavy smell she associated with Jean's cigars but a clean, sweet scent. Like freshly cut grass in summer, only richer. His mouth had tasted of it faintly the night of their kiss.

The sound of a match striking drew her attention across the room and soon Gray's profile was lit by the glow of an oil lamp. Her eyes widened when the light also illuminated the bed beside him.

His bed. It was small. Little more than a cot, but neatly made with clean linens.

A strange tingle began to flicker within her, much like it had the night he had taken her home. Unlike her room, which had been decorated from catalogs and christened with the comings and goings of maids and occasionally her uncle and Monsieur Sinclair when he retrieved her jewelry, Gray's room was intimate in its scarcity and isolation. Everything in it had been imbued with his essence, free from the dilution of other hands.

It was *too* intimate.

He seemed to feel it, too, and avoided her gaze as he straightened and removed his coat and hat. Then he walked around her and hung both on a set of pegs by the door. Bereft of words, she followed his lead and removed her hat with its annoying veil. It didn't seem to belong on a peg, though, so she walked the few steps necessary to reach the small table near the single window and set it there. The window was completely covered in a heavy, dark fabric that eliminated all light and most of the sound from the street, further adding to the feeling of intimacy.

"Here." He turned with his hand outstretched to her.

"Oh." She recognized the bills that Jeb had pushed across the table. "Thank you." She managed to take them without touching his hand and was about to push them uncounted into her reticule but thought better of it and slowly spread them out in her hands. "That bastard." She muttered, thinking of Jeb, and stuffed them in. It was less than half the amount she'd started with.

"For what it's worth, you're a damn fine player. You won the first game fairly."

Sophie looked up to see him smiling at her in a way she had never seen from him before. Relaxed in his own environment, his even, white teeth shone brightly in contrast with his golden-brown skin and his eyes softened, losing a good bit of their usual solemnity. The effect quite literally made it difficult for her to breathe, so she looked back down under the pretense of tying the drawstring closed on her bag. "M-Monsieur Sinclair taught me to play. Last winter was so cold there was plenty of time—" The full meaning of his words registered. "Wait? You were there, in the gaming hall, from the beginning?" Her gaze flew up to his, suddenly recovered from her temporary bout of bashfulness.

He nodded, looking a bit too smug for her taste. "I followed you from the dress shop."

"Why did you let me get so far then?"

He sobered a bit and seemed reluctant to speak, the muscles

of his throat working before he finally answered. "Because I wanted to watch you."

The statement touched her like a caress, stealing her words again. It could have been benign, a simple curiosity to know how she played, but the nuance of his tone suggested it wasn't. She felt cowardly as she did it, but she looked away again, her eyes flitting between the single chair, the neat row of hooks that held his extra shirts and pants, the bedside table, the bed.

"You'll be safe here."

She blushed because she knew he saw her looking at the bed and guessed he was thinking about their kiss. "Why am I here?"

"Beaudin's men. We didn't think they saw you leave the dress shop, so Sinclair took Martine home in your place. We can't risk sneaking you back tonight. We'll go back to the dress shop in the morning, and you can leave for home from there."

They were helping her hide this transgression from Jean. A moment of giddiness overcame her and almost escaped up her throat in a laugh. She covered her mouth with her hand to keep it in.

Martine was only a few years older than herself with similar coloring, so she hoped the plan would work. But she thought of the other woman alone with Monsieur Sinclair and prayed that he wouldn't deal too harshly with her. But then she realized Gray's words meant she would be spending the night with him and her stomach twisted. It also put an end to her inexplicable giggles.

"Does that mean you won't tell Jean about this?" she asked.

"You deserve to have your arse tanned, but we won't tell him." He grinned.

"Then let me go now. Tell Monsieur Sinclair you couldn't find me."

"You won't get far if that's all the money you have." He gestured to her reticule, the teasing light vanished from his eyes. She was sorry to see it go.

Sophie opened her mouth to argue that she might have had more without his interference but recognized it for the childish inclination it was. He had probably saved her and the knowledge chaffed. Those men wouldn't have let her leave the gaming hall.

"Then help me get more. With you backing me up, Jeb wouldn't have tried to renege. I could get enough to go to Chicago and find my brother."

"You don't even know he's in Chicago."

"He went there after our parents died. Jean corresponds with him...." Her words died out when she realized her only contact with her brother had been through Jean. What if he wasn't in Chicago after all? Would Jean lie about that? Her heart sank. "Do you know where Alexandre is?" She asked very softly.

"No."

His answer was just as low and it wasn't a surprise. It should have driven home to Sophie how alone she really was, completely cut off from the one family connection she'd held on to, but it didn't. Because her brother had been lost to her for a long time and for some inexplicable reason, Gray made her feel safe.

"So you won't help me earn more money?"

"Sophie." Her name on his lips pleased her in ways it shouldn't have. "If you run, LaSalle will find you." Instead of being cold, his eyes were filled with tenderness and regret.

He was right. She meant to be angry at his words, but his eyes thwarted her. She knew he was right, but now she also knew that maybe it pained him to be right.

"You're not like anyone else." Sophie finally gave voice to the secret conversation they always seemed to have when they looked at each other. The words had never been spoken, but they had always been there between them.

Gray's eyes cut to the left, away from her, and a muscle worked in his jaw. He didn't want to give voice to the undercurrent that carried between them, but he couldn't deny its existence. Heartened by his reaction, she took the few steps that would bring her to within arm's reach of him.

His solemn gaze moved back to her face, the intensity brushing across each feature like a caress until coming to rest on her mouth. Something responded deep inside her. She always felt so safe with him but now there was a hint of something else, something dangerous and exciting. Something more. She longed to explore it.

When his gaze moved back up to hers, full of fire and hunger, she knew he felt it, too. He'd looked at her exactly the same way the night of their kiss. She wanted to experience that kiss again. To experience those feelings he could stir to life within her. If it turned out she had to go to Anton's bed, she could take that with her.

"If I wanted to kiss you again, would you let me?"

His eyes flared in surprise, and she heard him suck in a quick breath. "You're very bold."

Her face burned and she silently acknowledged the truth of his words. The reckless streak in her did seem to be running rampant lately, but she attributed it to the fact that her life would be ending in two weeks. Surely this is how people felt when they knew the end was near. Heedless of consequence and irresponsible of judgment. For what consequence could be worse than marrying Anton Beaudin?

"I know." Her brow furrowed. "But you want me, too. Don't you?"

There was no hesitation in his answer. "More than anything. But you don't know what you're asking."

"We did kiss once." Her lips curved in a soft smile at the memory, but she had to look down at her hands, away from him. "You liked it. I think I remember what it involves."

"What you remember happened in your room where anybody could've walked in on us. And still it went too far." His voice was tense. "No one would see this kiss," he added with meaning.

"Isn't that a good thing?"

Gray's breath came out in a long sigh and he rubbed a frustrated hand over his face. "It's bad, Sophie. So bad." Instead of looking at her, he chose a spot on the wall over her shoulder. "Just go to sleep. I can't talk about this with you."

Her lips parted in surprise and, despite his best attempts, Gray looked at them. She looked so unhappy and dejected he wanted to take his words back. To pull her into his arms, bear her down to the bed beneath him and lose himself in her until those eyes were too full of passion to look sad. And then he wanted to take her away. Ride with her across the plains until it was just the two of them and never look back.

Damn! What had he been thinking to bring her here? His obsession couldn't withstand the temptation of having her so close. One kiss here and he'd it all from her.

"It's too early to sleep."

"Just go to sleep." He repeated through clenched teeth.

She looked miffed when her fingers came up to begin unfastening the buttons on her jacket.

"Whoa! What the hell are you doing?"

"You try sleeping in a corset and bustle." She snapped, undeterred in her objective.

His sense of self-preservation made him do what he had never done to another human being in his adult life. He turned his

55

back on her. But still he couldn't take his eyes *from* her and they immediately strayed to the small shaving mirror mounted on the wall a few feet away. It wasn't big and it was cracked through the middle, but it was enough.

Gray watched in acute discomfort, clenching his fists at his sides, as Sophie slowly revealed herself to him. When she unbuttoned the jacket, she exposed creamy shoulders and a chemise that was far too sheer. His mouth went dry when he noticed the darker hint of areolas peeking just above her corset. She threw the jacket over the back of the chair and then moved on to her skirt. He watched her fidget with the tie and knew a second of madness when he had to stop himself from tearing it apart for her. Moments later she stepped out of it and it was soon followed by petticoats and bustle. He broke out in a sweat when she began the laces of her corset and had to look away. Only to look back as she sat on the edge of the bed to remove her ankle boots and stockings, unveiling shapely, pale calves and a pair of dainty feet.

Dressed in only her drawers and chemise, she stood and began the agonizingly slow process of taking the pins from her hair. He tried not to but his gaze strayed down to the apex of her thighs where he could just make out the shadow of curls scarcely hidden by the too-thin linen of her drawers. He felt himself harden and made himself look away. But the hairpins clinked one by one to the bedside table and when they stopped his gaze darted back in time to see her glorious mane, shining gold in the lamplight, fall down to her waist.

The chemise mocked his discomfort and dropped off either shoulder, baring an indecent amount of soft, smooth flesh when she bent over to move her shoes out of the way. He closed his eyes and pretended he hadn't just seen the lush, unrestrained curves of her breasts. But the memory of her nipple, pink and bared to his gaze and mouth, flashed through his mind. If he hadn't been fully hard before, he was now.

"Gray?" Her soft voice carried to him.

Gray waited until he got himself under control. "What?" He finally bit out between clenched teeth.

He opened his eyes. In the mirror he could see that she had paused, one knee resting on the bed, chemise drooping dangerously low to reveal the upper swells of her ripe breasts, the very image of an innocent seductress, until his gaze met hers looking back at him in the mirror.

So she knew he'd been watching her, he realized. And something wild broke free within him.

"I...I wouldn't tell anyone..." She began.

His blood, already hot and heavy in his loins, roared through him with such savage energy Gray knew he was powerless to resist its urging. He had just lost whatever tenuous hold he had on rational thought.

"Ah, hell," he growled.

In the space of a heartbeat, he damned the consequences and crossed the room to reach her.

Chapter Eight

The stark need in his eyes as he approached might have filled Sophie with apprehension had she had the time to process it before Gray pulled her into his arms. But he moved so fast she barely had time to keep her heart from exploding from her chest before his mouth covered hers. His fingers gripped her arms and pulled her tight against him as he plundered her. His tongue pushed inside, mating with hers with an insistency that caused such an immediate, responsive arousal in her that it left her breathless.

Sophie loved the solid press of his chest against her breasts and moved her palms against the hard planes as they made their way to his shoulders and then up so her fingers curled around his neck and twined in the silk of his hair. She loved his hair and had been aching to plunge her fingers into the richness. But they couldn't stay still. There was too much of him to explore. They greedily sought to cup his strong jaw as it moved with his kiss before moving back down to curl around the breadth of his back and pull him closer.

He groaned low in his throat and dropped his hands to fill them with the fleshy globes of her nearly naked bottom. Sophie marveled at the languorous heaviness that settled low in her belly in response. Then he squeezed hard and she broke the kiss to gasp at the thrill that shot through her groin. An answering flood of heat pooled between her thighs. His hot breath fanned her lips, sending sparks of electricity prickling across her face. His lips brushed hers, but softer this time, and then she was moving backward in a controlled fall that ended with him raised above her on the bed.

She opened her eyes to question him but was caught in the intensity that met her gaze.

"You've been kissed. Now go to sleep." And he pushed himself off of her to flop on his back beside her.

Sophie laid there breathing heavily, trying to come to terms with what was happening to her body. She knew he was right to stop, and was fairly certain what the pulsing of her body meant, but she didn't care. It became clear to her that everything had been building to this. She should be angry with him for not helping her escape. She should hate him for thwarting her. But those thoughts had hardly even raised their heads.

So she closed her eyes and laid there by his side until she could get herself under control. It didn't help that the bed was so small he was pressed against her from shoulder to hip, that his scent permeated her senses and refused to let her calm down. But finally she felt herself return to some measure of normalcy and she rolled on her side to give him more room while raising herself on an elbow to look down at him.

He lay there with an arm thrown over his eyes and she noticed, with quite a bit of pleasure, that he was still breathing heavily. She took note of the strange band of leather tied around his wrist, wondering what it meant. Her appreciative gaze traveled over the rest of him until it came to a stop on the hand that rested on his stomach. Before she could stop herself, she reached for his gracefully long fingers and brought them to her lips.

His eyes jerked to her then and she smiled as she met them. "Thank you for the kiss." She did not relinquish his hand and in response his fingers curled around her own. "Thank you for stopping, too. I never knew you were such a gentleman." She teased.

"I'm not." He was not teasing. "You're innocent. I wouldn't take that from you."

Sophie thought about that for a while. Yes, she was innocent, strictly speaking. But he'd made her feel things innocents were probably not supposed to feel and she suspected those feelings to be rare. Feelings she may never have again. Particularly if she escaped, which she had every intention of attempting, and especially if the worst happened and she married Anton. This night had been given to them as a gift, maybe she'd realized it even as he'd led her away from the gaming hall. It was their one night to explore what was between them. Their only night. She'd be a fool to let it pass. If she escaped, it would be a nice memory, if she went to Anton, it would be the only thing she could keep of her own. Anton was expecting a virgin, but she'd deal with that later. Maybe he'd divorce her, she mused.

"What if I gave it to you?"

Gray went stone still as the words settled between them. She watched his face as he processed them and held her breath. Her heart fluttered in her chest when he turned and rose on his elbow in a pose identical to hers. But he was bigger, so she had to look up at him.

"Are you?" he asked.

His husky voice raked her skin, sucking the air from the room. The heat emanating from his body made her feel too hot. Along with her heart palpitations, it left her momentarily dumbstruck. "W-what?" she finally managed to stutter.

"Are you giving me your innocence?" His thumb brushed her knuckles in a light caress that left them tingling.

"Yes," she whispered. It seemed inappropriate to say the word too loudly.

His breath warmed her cheek as he breathed slowly in and out. But his gaze had left her face to settle on their joined hands. "You don't know how often I've thought about it."

"You've thought about me?"

He nodded. "I've thought about how I want to take you away. How I want to disappear with you so you'd be mine." His gaze met hers after he said that and she felt its jolt all through her body.

His words set off a spark within her and momentary bout of bashfulness began to fade away. She laid back and his hand automatically moved to rest on her stomach. "So maybe for tonight we can pretend you have run away with me," she said.

Something deep and visceral crossed his face and his hand tightened in her chemise. It was her only warning before his mouth crushed hers.

"Ow!"

Gray pulled back immediately at her cry of pain. "Your gun," she explained in a whisper, already reaching to pull him back. It had dug painfully into the soft flesh of her hip.

Gray sat on his knees to untie the leather thong from his thigh and unbuckle his gun belt, hardly waiting for it to drop to the bare wood floor before he was on her again. His clothed body covering her almost naked one.

"Sorry," he whispered against her mouth.

She welcomed the weight of him on her and parted her lips to his kiss. His tongue swept into her mouth, filling her body with a new level of excitement because now she knew the kiss was only the beginning. But soon his lips left hers to brush hot, open-mouthed kisses across her cheekbone to the lobe of her ear and down her neck. A calloused hand moved roughly to push the chemise down her shoulder and then even lower until her nipple strained against the fabric briefly before pushing free. The hand immediately covered her lush breast and kneaded, surprisingly gentle despite his urgency. His thumb moved slowly over the pebbled tip.

Sophie arched into his touch. He was still kissing her neck but she remembered what his mouth felt like on her breast and wanted to feel it again. So she twined her fingers in his hair and pulled him down to the one he had just exposed to the night. His husky laughter caressed her skin, making it prickle, but he obliged and in moments she felt the moist heat of his mouth close over her. The tug of his lips brought about an immediate twinge of pleasure she felt deep in her core.

When his teeth scraped her, she arched involuntarily against him.

He responded by grinding his hips against her thigh. The hard ridge of his manhood pressed hot against her and she instinctively knew she wanted, needed, to get to that. Her hands left his hair and in moments one had found a gap between them and had moved down to feel him through the soft fabric of his pants.

"Ah, Sophie," he gasped against her skin.

She chewed her bottom lip and let her palm slide along the ridge, marveling at his length and how he responded to her touch. His hips bucked lightly against her stroke so she experimented with her power and squeezed gently, wringing a strangled cry of pleasure from him. But then he pressed himself firmly against her thigh, stopping any further play on her part.

"Don't stop, mon coeur. I need you."

His mouth took hers hard one more time before pulling away, stopping only to hook a finger in the second strap of her chemise and tug it down, exposing her other breast. Gray placed a tender kiss on the pink nipple before leaving her to sit on the edge of the bed.

His boots fell with two soft thuds onto the hard floor before he stood and worked the buttons of his shirt. His skin gleamed in the low light as he shrugged out of it and tossed it to the chair to join her pile of clothes. Sophie's lips parted in surprise when she saw the twin tattoos. They were various geometrical shapes etched in a black band around each of his biceps.

Shirtless, wearing nothing but his trousers, and with his hair hanging loose except for the one braid, he was beautiful. She moved to her knees in front of him, torn between wanting to see more of him and needing to touch what she had only imagined before. Her fingertips lightly trailed over the peaks and dips of his smooth chest before her palms dared to press against the warm flesh.

"You're so beautiful, Gray." If there was ever a finer specimen of a man's chest, she had not seen it. Not in any of the books on Grecian art she had studied or even on the occasional shirtless man she had seen at the stables. Or maybe it was only that this was Gray's chest and, somehow over the past months, he had become the standard by which all men were measured.

Her palms moved down over the hard ridges of his stomach, fascinated by how he was so different from her. Hard where she was soft. They came to a stop at the waistband of his pants and she felt him draw in a deep breath.

"Can I?" Her tentative blue eyes met his hot gray ones.

"You have to know I'm at your mercy." His intense gaze pierced hers.

She smiled and slowly pulled at the fastening. Her breath hitched when she saw the first sprinkling of dark hair. She pushed down but the pants caught. His hands came up to work them past his erection and then it sprang free, perfectly upright and reaching for his navel.

Sophie slowly reached for him, surprised and faintly apprehensive about his size. He was hot in her palm and jerked slightly when she held him. Steel encased with satin. A tiny bead of moisture gathered at the tip and she couldn't resist rubbing it with her thumb. She looked up to gauge his reaction.

"Lie back." His eyes had gone hooded and his voice brooked no argument, but she was more than willing to comply. Her insides felt like they had turned molten and she ached between her legs where before she had only felt tingles of awareness.

She should have been far past blushing but she felt herself do just that when Gray's fiery gaze devoured her before bracing a knee on the mattress and gripping her drawers. But he paused as her gaze met his.

"You knew I was watching you undress?" he asked.

She had the grace to smile sheepishly as she confessed, "I knew."

He smiled, too, a wicked, sinful thing, and tugged. She lifted her hips to help and her drawers quickly joined the growing pile of clothes on the chair.

"Gray." She squirmed now, wanting him in a way she couldn't name.

His face gave nothing away as his gaze raked her body before he slowly leaned down. His lips brushed her thighs and then placed a tender kiss on the golden curls at their apex. His fingers pushed up the cotton chemise so he could kiss her belly, tongue dipping into her navel, before placing an open-mouthed kiss of possession on each nipple and finally making his way to her mouth. She felt his urgency when his knee worked its way between her unresisting, but suddenly hesitant, thighs and he settled himself between them. *That* part of him seemed to have a life of its own and brushed against her.

"Look at me, Sophie." His words brought her gaze to his, only inches above her. He didn't smile, but his eyes were tender as his hand moved between them. Her eyes widened as she felt his fingers touch her where she ached and she would have closed her thighs except his body was between them. She gasped aloud when he suddenly sheathed a finger inside her. It intensified the aching there. She tried to move with his finger but his weight pressed her down so she only managed to grind herself against him. But, oh, the friction felt so good.

"You're so wet. So ready." He whispered in her ear just before taking the sensitive lobe between his teeth, causing her intimate muscles to tighten deliciously.

She *was* ready, more than ready. Sophie felt wanton as she bent her knees to put her feet flat on the bed so she could open her legs wider. His finger left her and then she felt that foreign part of him touching her. He flexed forward and pushed the head inside, just past the tight opening. The delicious heaviness of him there, hot and throbbing, parting her, made her arch to take him in farther. But he moved slowly, priming her with a few easy, shallow thrusts that stoked the tension inside her and made her moan to be filled.

Gray held back. And instead of taking her like she wanted, he raised himself on an elbow above her and moved his hand back to where they were barely joined and stroked her there. The pad of his thumb moved over the tender, distended flesh in a steady rhythm that slowly increased with her arousal. Sophie panted as her universe narrowed to that touch occasionally emphasized by the inadvertent jerk of his hips. She watched as a telling bead of sweat formed on his brow and lazily trickled down to his cheekbone, and wanted to lick it from his skin, before her eyes closed, too far gone in her own pleasure to think of anything except his touch. Then the tremors began. Starting slowly at the precious spot where his thumb worked and moving their way out through her whole body. She groaned when the first wave crested and held on tight as others came and washed over her.

Unable to hold back anymore, Gray sheathed himself completely inside her in a deep thrust, forcing the delicate tissue of her channel apart to accept his size. Sophie stiffened and made a noise low in her throat, her nails biting into his shoulders to stay him. He tried to hold back, to allow her untried body to get used to the feel of him, his whole body shaking with the effort, but he failed miserably. His fingertips bit into the soft flesh of her buttocks to hold her still for him as his hips grinded against her, unwilling to obey the commands of his mind.

She was so tight and hot wrapped around him, he only wanted to pound into her in a mindless fervor of abandon. And then she moved. A simple shift of position, probably, but his body took it as submission and before he could get a grip on his passion, he pulled back and pushed into her. A single, deep, mind-numbing in its intensity thrust that was in no way gentle and in all ways the raw hunger he was afraid to unleash on her.

"Shit, Sophie." He started to pull away from her. "I'm sorry," he whispered.

"Gray." From beneath him, her voice penetrated his consciousness and summoned his gaze to hers. "Don't leave!" She grabbed him desperately. "Please."

He didn't breathe as he looked down at her, hardly able to believe that he was hearing her correctly. That despite the pain he had caused her, she still wanted him. There was no fear on her face. She wanted him. To prove it she grabbed his hips and pulled him back into her.

"More."

And then her hips were arching up to him, attempting to set a rhythm and he was lost. He fell over her then, resting on his forearms, aware of her slim, delicate body beneath him. His hands were trembling as he fisted them in the sheet on either side of her. Slowly and with infinite gentleness, he pushed into her again, his gaze locked on her face until he was fully seated within her. Her passage was so incredibly tight he was sure he'd hurt her, but her eyes were heavy-lidded and glazed with passion when they met his. He pulled out of her almost completely, and smiled when her fingernails bit into his hips to pull him back. He obliged and tenderly thrust into her again.

"Please, Gray." Her hips rose, asking for more friction.

It was all the encouragement he needed. He drove into her then without restraint, giving into the madness of their passion, watching in awe as her face changed with each stroke. Finally her hoarse cry filled the room and he watched her come apart, felt her come apart, as she contracted around his shaft. Only then did he bury his face in her neck and hold her tight until his own groan of pleasure tore itself from his lips. He barely managed to pull out of her before spilling his seed.

He fell onto her then, limp and sated, and sure that she had taken some part of his soul.

Long moments passed in silence as their breathing returned

to normal. Sophie relished the way his body felt, completely relaxed and calm, on top of her. But he stirred then and shifted so the bulk of him lay beside her, a heavy thigh still positioned between hers and his shoulder still covering most of her torso. The air in the room was so warm their skin glistened in the meager lamp light, but it didn't matter. She savored him and the slick feel of his skin on hers.

"Are you okay?"

Sophie opened her eyes to see him raised slightly, gaze roving her face in search of damage. As if any damage he'd caused would be visible on her face, she mused. "Wonderful, mon coeur." Her fingertips caressed his cheek and he reflexively turned to press a kiss to the center of her palm.

Her other hand came up to stroke his shoulder and then down to trace lightly over the tattoo, overwhelmed by her need to touch him, to somehow be closer to him even though they had just completed an act that brought them as close as two people could physically be.

"Is it always this way?" she whispered, hoping he didn't need clarification because she wasn't quite sure how to express the complex feelings of longing and completeness she felt.

When his gaze met hers again the solemnity was back but there was something else. And when he whispered "never" Sophie's breath caught in her throat. She realized, more than anything else, she wanted to see him look at her like that every day for the rest of her life. But there were so many things in the way.

"I'm sorry if I made you do something you didn't want to," she blurted out.

He laughed. A soft exhalation of air that caused prickles of pleasure to dance across her skin where it touched as he bent and placed a kiss on her shoulder, her chest, her neck, just before his lips brushed across hers. "Did it feel like you had an unwilling man between your thighs?"

Her cheeks pinkened. "No. I meant..." Her voice faded. It didn't seem right to mention her uncle, Anton, and Gray's profession. Those things had no place in the room with them anymore.

But he knew.

"We have tonight, Sophie." And he kissed her again. A slow, deep, wet kiss that made that part of her start to ache again. When he pulled back there was a devious glint in his eyes that promised to make good use of the hours ahead.

Chapter Nine

S ome time later, Gray lay with Sophie curled against his chest. One hand gripped her hip in a mildly possessive touch while the fingers of his other hand were threaded with hers. The pose seemed so natural, it scared the hell out of him.

She'd just finished telling him about her childhood. The ranch, her parents, her brother, and how happy they'd been. Perfectly idyllic until LaSalle had come and convinced her father to mine their land. She didn't mention that part but Sinclair had told him about his suspicions. When the mine began showing profit, her parents had been killed in an accident that LaSalle had almost certainly arranged. He wondered if she knew about that. The thought of Sophie at her uncle's mercy filled him with a rage that bordered on uncontrollable. He wanted to protect her no matter the cost.

She rose up to look down at their clasped hands. He swallowed hard at the smile she bestowed on him. Her heart was reflected in that smile, and it made him ache because he had no idea how to keep that heart from breaking come morning. He had no idea how he would let her go, for that matter, so he pushed the thought from his mind and squeezed her close. They had tonight.

"Any regrets?" Her voice was as soft as the lighting.

"Never." He couldn't stop himself from smiling back. Even he was surprised at how true it was. No matter what happened, he would remember this night with her for the rest of his life.

"Now that you've thoroughly ravished me, will you tell me about yourself?"

He laughed. "I'm not interesting."

"You are. Tell me." She folded her hands on his chest and rested her chin there, waiting.

It ran counter to his nature to talk about himself so he started with the most recent things and worked backward. He told her about how he worked at Victoria House before coming to work for LaSalle, and the ranch he'd worked at before that tracking horse thieves. When he opened his mouth to tell her about the job before that, she started laughing.

"What's so funny?" And he rolled so that he hovered above her.

"You don't talk about yourself much, do you?" she managed

between chuckles. "I don't care about your profession, your life as a gunman or gunslinger or whatever you call yourself. I want to know about *you*."

"You should know better than to ask people out here about themselves." He was only half kidding. This is where everyone came to start over.

"But you're not *people*, you're Gray." She looked at him as if that meant something to her.

The sudden lump in his throat made it difficult to answer. He brushed his thumb across her cheekbone, admiring how the shadows played beneath it. "Nobody's ever asked about me."

"No one? There hasn't been one woman in your past?"

So that's what she was getting at. He shook his head and took a breath before he answered, knowing she probably wouldn't like what he had to say, but she deserved honesty—as much as he was able—so that's what he gave her. "No one I haven't paid."

The smile was gone from her lovely face. "Have there only been...prostitutes?"

"I move from job to job, town to town, and it doesn't leave a lot of time for women. After a while, I stopped thinking of any sort of future." Looking into her face, that had all changed. Glimpses of what might be shoved themselves into his head. Sharing meals at a table. Laughing together as they walked hand in hand. "I haven't lain with a woman in a long time, Sophie."

Now that he knew the joy of pleasuring Sophie he wondered if sex with another woman would ever be satisfying again.

She surprised him again by kissing him. "How a man like you has walked God's green earth and not managed to have at least one woman fall in love with him is beyond me."

He closed his eyes against the simple pleasure he found in her words. It would be so easy to love her. If only LaSalle didn't stand between them, and he didn't owe a debt to Sinclair. He rested his head on her breasts, listening to her heart thrum. "It doesn't matter."

"What about your family? Your parents."

"Let's not talk about me anymore."

"Please?" she asked sweetly and brushed a hand over his hair.

He lifted up to stare into the deep blue pools of her eyes and understood the need she felt. The need to remove all barriers between them, even if it was just for the night.

"Dead. They've been gone for a long time. There's only me."

He'd never felt he belonged anywhere. The only acceptance he'd found had come in the form of the cash men paid for his gun...until now...until her. He wanted to find the words to tell her, but after so many years they wouldn't come. It wouldn't be fair to her anyway. He couldn't tell her the full truth of who he was. When she found out, she might hate him anyway.

"We're both alone," she whispered, her hand cool on his cheek.

He closed his eyes and put his head back down, lulled by the steady beat of her heart as her fingers played in his hair.

"I'm sorry for what you've gone through, mon coeur. But I'm

thankful for whatever has led you to me."

"Me too," he whispered.

And he meant it.

Just as the first yellow streaks of dawn were peeking around the curtain, Sophie succumbed to the exhaustion of the night spent making love and closed her eyes. When she opened them again, Gray was dressed and leaning over her, his eyes tender.

She begged for more sleep but when he moved into bed beside her and held her close, she was afraid to close her eyes. Afraid to lose any more time with him. So they fed each other breakfast in bed—the buttermilk biscuits, bacon, and coffee he had gone out to get while she slept.

Only after she finally convinced him to turn his back did she get out of bed and wash with the pitcher of water he'd brought. It had gone cold by then but it was worth the extra time spent in bed with him. She couldn't stop thinking about the things they had done to each other throughout the night, the things he had confessed to her, and she savored the languorous feeling of contentment that she took with her. Until she felt his arms snake around her hips and pull her back to him.

"Gray!" She meant to scold but it came out as a laugh and then she felt a suspicious hardness strain his pants and press against her buttocks. "God, you're insatiable."

"I can't get enough of you." He smiled against her neck.

"If only I wasn't so sore." She'd lost track of how many times he'd been inside her and knew she'd be tender for weeks as it was.

"I'm not sorry for that."

"Beast," she accused as she turned in his arms and wrapped hers around his shoulders.

He growled and kissed her until reluctantly pulling back to retrieve her clothes. He even helped her dress, kissing each body part before he covered it. Once she was fully dressed the mood changed subtly, and the reality they had tried so hard to keep at bay slowly began to infiltrate their nest. When she turned from the shaving mirror, finished with her hair, he grabbed her hand and silently pulled her down onto his lap in the chair.

She curled into him and buried her face in his neck, breathing deeply of his scent while some invisible clock ticked away their last minutes together. Even now, with only moments left in their solitude, she was reluctant to ruin it with talk of what might happen. But she knew it must be discussed. There would be no time alone once they met Monsieur Sinclair and Martine at the dress shop.

"Gray, I..." His thumb, all this time absently stroking a stray lock of her hair, stilled. She watched him gently disentangle his hand and move it to grip the arm of the chair. Her gaze turned then to find his, to understand why he had suddenly gone stiff. But he only looked at her, giving nothing away. She recognized it as the facade she often wore herself, a wall between them, and it scared her like nothing else could, but she persisted.

"How do we go on from here? I can't imagine...I don't want to go on without this—without you."

He didn't say anything. They gray of his eyes had turned to steel.

Her stomach twisted in fear, but she had to say it. She could not go the rest of her life without saying it. "I've never felt about anyone else the way I feel about you. I want to be with you." *I think I could love you.* There was no time left. It was now or never. "I think I—"

He flinched when she touched his cheek, throwing cold water on the words lodged in her throat. The chill worked its way to her extremities until her fingertips were numb with it, and her hand dropped uselessly to her lap.

"There has to be a wedding, Sophie." The words only confirmed what his face had told her. She barely felt it as he gently took hold of her and set her on her feet.

"I don't understand," she finally managed in a near whisper.

He was standing then, close enough to touch, but their arms stayed firmly at their sides. She watched him open and close his mouth several times in an effort to gather his thoughts. Finally he spoke, but it fell pathetically short of what she needed to hear. "We had last night." He did seem regretful as he spoke and touched a wisp of her hair. "I can't promise you anything. I never promised you more. Please." He dropped his hand and took in a deep breath.

"Please?" The expression of resigned regret he wore did nothing to soothe her. "Please what?" For the life of her she had no idea what he was asking or wanting from her. She could not accept what he was telling her, could not accept that he was ready to move on. Each time they had made love it had been more achingly tender than the last.

"Don't ask more of me." His voice was low, aching.

As reality came crashing down, she realized the possible consequences of their night and her hand instinctively went to her belly.

"Don't worry," he quickly reassured her, correctly interpreting her action. "I never spilled my seed in you."

She jerked as if he had slapped her. She was thankful he had thought to ensure there would be no child to consider, but it was a harsh reminder that he had been thinking of this moment when he would say goodbye to her all along. Which, of course he had been, the night wasn't supposed to be anything more.

She was the fool here. She was the one trying to make more of it than it was.

His hands were on her shoulders. "Sophie, don't be mad. I would change things if I could."

What he meant by that statement she didn't know or care to take the time to figure out. She whirled away from him and quickly settled the veiled hat on her head. The room had become stifling, and she needed to get away from him.

"I understand." She managed to keep her voice steady. "I

wouldn't ask you to face my uncle." And she didn't want him to face Jean. He'd only be hurt or, more likely, killed. It was best this way. This way she was the only one hurt.

She fled down the stairs and blindly made her way back to the dress shop. She knew he shadowed her by only a few steps, but she did her best not to look at him. Anton Beaudin was her future and she cursed herself every kind of fool for forgetting it even for a moment.

Only the strength of his iron will kept Gray from pulling Sophie to him and refusing to let her go. He wanted her in his life. Hell, he'd acknowledged that from the moment he'd watched her come apart in his arms. Being with her had given him a sense of redemption, of life, of what it would be to love and have a future. What it meant to be accepted. No one had ever looked at him with the love and acceptance she had shown him. But he had a job to do and that had to come first, because if he didn't put it first they would have no chance at all.

If only he could tell her all of that. He couldn't take the risk she might reveal their plan. His only choice was to endure her hate until the wedding and beg her forgiveness after.

And hope that everything went according to plan and she didn't end up married to Beaudin.

Chapter Ten

Sophie closed her eyes and held her face up to the cool wind that blew in from across the valley, doing her best to settle her nerves for the drop that was ahead of her. She perched on her knees by the open window of her bedroom and slowly opened her eyes to look down. Her bedroom faced the back of the house and the roof of the sunroom was just below. It was only a short drop down and then another to the ground.

The tricky part would come when she attempted to purchase a ticket for the stagecoach. She'd already determined the schedule from an ad in the newspaper. It was leaving in the morning at six o'clock—too early for her absence to be noted and Jean wasn't due back home until the next day. Her anxious gaze looked out in the distance, knowing that the train tracks were somewhere out there. Taking the train would be infinitely faster if only she had the funds.

There were only a few days until the wedding, and this very well might be her last chance of escape. Jean didn't have any plans to travel after this trip, because his friends would be coming into town to stay with them for the wedding.

She picked up her wool valise, which contained her extra clothes and the few pieces of silver she had pilfered from the dining room, and held her breath as she dropped it out the window. It landed softly on the roof below and no one came running. Good. If all went to plan, she would be on the coach in a few hours with no one being the wiser. Her only regret was that it would mean leaving Gray behind. She had not cried for him after the first day, not that those tears had served her any purpose, anyway. The ache that had lodged itself firmly in her chest was still present and she feared it wouldn't be leaving anytime soon. She was doomed to lose him.

She wanted to hate him, and there were times she almost succeeded. He had taken her virtue—well, had it foisted upon him—and coldly brushed her aside in no uncertain terms. Only he hadn't done it coldly. She could still remember the pain in his voice when he had touched her, pleaded with her, just before she had stormed from his room. He hadn't wanted to part with her. She was sure of it. He did feel *something* for her. But he had never promised her anything more. He'd never lied to her about that, she would give him that. It was her own foolishness that had dreamed something more could come from their one night together.

Was it his fault that he was at Jean's mercy just like everyone else? No, her reason screamed at her, but her heart felt betrayed. Why couldn't they leave together? Why couldn't he offer to go with her?

Stupid questions, those. She could not expect him to give up his entire life for her. Still, every time she saw Gray, she forgave him a little more. And she did see him. Almost daily, but never alone. Never so she could ask him those questions. She would catch him watching her with that solemn gaze, usually giving nothing away, but occasionally touching on the forlorn. She tried not to return his looks but it had become increasingly difficult since the initial heat of her anger had died out, and besides, looking at him soothed the pain left behind. A couple of times she had tried to approach him, but Monsieur Sinclair had come from nowhere and headed her off with a summons from Jean. It had often enough that it occurred to her then that Monsieur Sinclair might suspect that something had happened between them. Then she realized it didn't matter as long as Jean didn't know. She had even gone by Jean's study a few times, in the hopes that Gray would be posted there, but it was always one of the others. So she had concluded he was avoiding her and stopped trying.

Pushing thoughts of him aside, she hoisted herself through the open window, one leg at a time, until she dangled from the windowsill on her forearms. Her feet were still too far away to reach the roof below so she'd have to drop. Which would be fine, except she couldn't figure out how to close the window behind her. The fingers of one hand wrapped around the sash from the bottom but it refused to budge as she'd suspected it would. It had been difficult enough to open with both hands from inside. Finally, she gave up. Besides, it was well after midnight, no one would see it anyway.

She held tight to the sill and dropped until her arms were fully extended, then let go. She would have landed just fine, she was certain of it, but an arm caught her around the waist and a hand covered her mouth. That frightened her worse than the fall ever could have. But almost immediately, she recognized the breadth of the chest against her back and the scent that enveloped her.

"It's me." His breath whispered past her ear, making her skin come alive in awareness.

Her body sagged against him in relief as she tried to overcome the rush of adrenaline that pounded through her. "What are you doing on the roof?" The question came out of her in a breathless rush once he dropped the hand covering her mouth.

Gray didn't answer, though, he just held her against him until her heart stopped threatening to pound out of her chest. Finally, he moved away from her and explained. "I watch your window every night. I knew it was only a matter of time before you made a run for it." And then he picked up her valise and took her hand, leading her along the wall to the inverted corner where the sunroom met the rest of the house. Once there, he tossed the valise down and leaped nimbly down to the ground behind it. Sophie followed but much more hesitantly, getting down to her belly first and following that way. He caught her hips from behind and helped her reach the ground. But when he grabbed her hand again to pull her away, she revolted.

"What are you doing?"

"Taking you back upstairs before somebody sees you." He explained.

She pitched her voice low, and stated very firmly, "But I'm escaping. I'm not going back in. How can you want me to go back in there?"

He sighed but she couldn't see his face in the dark to see what that meant. "How far do you think you'd get?"

She honestly didn't know but it would be better than not trying. "How can you want me to go back in there knowing it means marriage to Anton? Is that what you want for me?"

As soon as the question left her lips, she was in his arms with his face buried in her hair. "No, the thought of you with him eats me up inside." His voice was harsh against her ear.

Sophie savored the feel of his body against her, warm and comforting and so incredibly right it shouldn't be forbidden. "Then let me go," she whispered. "I could...I could wait for you or...or you could come with me." Before she'd even finished she could feel him shaking his head exactly as she had known he would.

"I can't come with you. It has to be this way. Trust me."

"Trust you?" It was an alarming concept. Jean had made it so she wasn't sure she could ever trust anyone. Yet, there was something in his words. Something more that he couldn't, or wouldn't, say. Sophie pulled back just far enough to look up at him but it was too dark to see much except the shadowed outline of his features. "Are you saying I won't have to marry Anton?"

He stared down at her and his thumb brushed her cheekbone, making the flesh there prickle with pleasure. "I'm saying you have to trust me." His voice was warm and intimate. It reminded her of how he had talked to her that night in his bed.

"What is going to happen? What's going on?"

"I can't say. I've already said too much."

The statement made her stomach flip-flop with anxiety. Could she trust him? He hadn't told Jean the truth about that night but that could be because it saved him as much as it did her. How could she trust him when she didn't even know what that meant? "Kiss me."

There was no hesitation from him and in seconds his lips were on hers. The kiss was soft and tender, everything she imagined a goodbye kiss should be, but then he pressed inside and it became a kiss of hunger and promise that left her knees weak and made her lean heavily against him for support. When he released her, his hands held her face and his nose brushed hers. "Just trust me, Sophie. Please."

And God help her, she did.

Chapter Eleven

T he day of the wedding dawned dark with thunderclouds and a persistent chance of rain, in perfect accord with Sophie's mood. She clutched her pillow tighter and stared out the window into one of the clouds as it drifted slowly by, reminding her of Gray's eyes. Though she'd done nothing but think about it since he'd brought her back to her room, she hadn't been able to figure out what he was planning.

What did it mean to trust him? Was he intending to stop the wedding? It would happen in mere hours if he didn't stop it. Was that part of his plan? Or had he simply been trying to get her to go back to her room? Who was he anyway?

In an attempt to answer that last question, she had peppered Monsieur Sinclair with questions about Gray. He had been unsurprisingly evasive, which only added to her list of questions. She had let the matter drop, however, not wanting to interfere with whatever Gray had in mind...assuming it was anything and she wasn't a fool for being led back to her room like a good little lamb.

She didn't know and it left her gripping her pillow with white-knuckled terror. She'd already determined that, no matter what, her participation in the wedding would be forced. She could not bring herself to marry Anton willingly. The words that would bind her to that man forever would never come forth from her lips. In the end, though, it wouldn't matter. Jean would pay a bribe and it would be done, but at least she would know she had not married him in the eyes of God.

Her gaze moved from the cloud to the gown hanging in the corner and she felt her heart wrench. It really was a beautiful piece of work, just the sort of thing she had once dreamed of wearing to her wedding. White satin, with understated elegance and a few pieces of lace in all the right places. Now, if only the groom were right. She closed her eyes and without even trying, Gray stood there in his place. It was a foolish thought. He'd never want to marry her. Would he? She just didn't know what he felt and it was making her irrational. As she was trying to figure it out, there was a soft knock at the door.

Before she could get her hopes up that Gray might have come, Martine walked in. "I brought your breakfast."

"I'm not hungry."

Martine sighed, but didn't comment as she set the tray aside. "Well, we should get started then."

Sophie felt her stomach drop, but she nodded. The wedding would be at eleven sharp, downstairs in the parlor. If Gray had something planned, as the small hope flickering in the deepest recesses of her irrational mind insisted he did, then she wouldn't ruin it by making Jean suspicious. So she sat demurely in front of her dressing table while Martine fixed her hair, but all the while thinking of the way Gray had kissed her in that very same spot.

"It looks beautiful, if I do say so myself." Martine smiled and admired her handiwork.

Startled that enough time had passed for her hair to already be finished, Sophie shook herself from her reverie to look in the mirror. The coiffure did look beautiful. Her golden locks were pulled back from her face and pinned, but a strand of diamonds intermingled with baby's breath hid the pins and created a sort of tiara. The rest had been pulled back loosely so several curled strands fell down around her shoulders. "It's wonderful." But her gaze went back to the diamonds and she wondered bitterly if Jean would appear at Anton's tonight to demand them back.

The thought of the night ahead made her shudder and she caught sight of her face. It was drawn and pale with blue smudges beneath the eyes. She decided then on no cosmetics. Her face looked a horror and it would serve Jean and Anton right if that's the bride they got.

"We should put on your gown now," Martine prompted, hesitating. "I'll get Anne to help."

"No!" Sophie couldn't bear the company of anyone else. "We can do it alone."

Minutes later, it was finished and Martine excused herself to go downstairs. Sophie had half an hour to herself before the wedding.

The front bell had been ringing for the past hour as guests arrived. All of them important business associates and contacts Jean could finagle to accept the invitation. He had even invited his nemesis in the copper business, Tanner Jameson. It was best to maintain the appearance of a civil acquaintance, even though Sophie knew her uncle lamented the fact that he couldn't get his hands on their mines, and he'd once even considered marrying her to Mr. Jameson's son, Hunter, to accomplish it. She wouldn't put it past him to somehow try to plan an accident for the father and his heirs one day, so he could buy up their land at auction.

As if she needed any further proof that she was simply a pawn in this arrangement. She paced relentlessly, uncertain but hopeful that at any moment Gray would appear in her room and tell her everything would be fine, that she wouldn't have to marry Anton.

But the clock in her room ticked away without a knock on her door, without Gray, until finally it chimed eleven o'clock. She rubbed her damp palms on her gown, heedless of ruining it. It didn't matter. Nothing mattered if this damned wedding happened, if Gray had betrayed her.

She walked to the window, hoping to see some hope of escape. There was nothing. A cart loaded with hay was being driven by an old man and pulled by two tired horses on the street past the back wall of their garden. A woman walked with a child skipping ahead of her. Out there, life continued, while here inside, hers was ending.

At exactly ten minutes past the hour, a knock sounded lightly on her door. Sophie's heart leaped into her throat and pounded out a heavy rhythm. She approached it cautiously, even timidly, afraid to open it and see that it wasn't Gray. But finally her cold fingers turned the knob, and she had to stop her knees from going out, from giving in to the visceral response that instantly threatened to destroy her when she saw Martine's petite frame standing there. Not Gray. Her eyes fell closed and she leaned against the door frame as she finally allowed herself to admit his betrayal.

He wasn't coming. There would be no white knight riding to her rescue, no hero to keep her dragons at bay.

The physical pain that tore through her was worse than she could have imagined. It was as real as any knife wound and it left her trembling with the aftershocks. It was made even worse by the knowledge that she'd walked right into the betrayal, had known the danger in trusting anyone and had done it anyway. Had wanted so much to have someone to hold on to when she had known all along that the only person she'd ever really have was herself.

Immediately her thoughts went to the day, the night, the life ahead of her. And she knew, without any doubt, that giving herself to Gray had been the worst mistake of her life. Not because she was ashamed, but because it would make whatever happened with Anton so much worse. To have a taste of how things might have been and to lose it to settle for something that paled so much in comparison was worse than to have never known it at all.

"It's time. Monsieur LaSalle requests you to come now."

Sophie heard the words, but could barely nod a response past the pain that clogged her throat and threatened to cut off her air. In fact, she couldn't move at all until Martine reached out to gently take her hand. She squeezed in reassurance and pulled her into the hallway and toward the stairs. Sophie followed on wooden legs, barely aware of their progress until they reached the bottom and Jean stood there smiling.

But as he looked her over, his smile faded to a sneer of disappointment. No, this was not the painted doll-bride he had ordered. "Didn't you have enough time to get ready?" His hard gaze looked around the wide hallway to make sure they were alone.

No one was there except Martine behind her and Monsieur Sinclair standing sentry at the closed double doors of the parlor. He refrained from meeting her gaze as she looked at him. She looked past him to the doors, the voices coming from inside telling her it was filled with guests awaiting her arrival. Her stomach rolled and it was only the fact that she hadn't eaten anything that kept it from revolting.

"Go back upstairs and finish." His voice snapped against her like a whip.

"So you think the lamb should go to the slaughter peacefully?" Her voice was raw as it scraped past the lump in her throat.

"Martine, get the flowers." His fingers bit into her arm as he pulled her toward the closed doors. His voice lowered, but she felt its venom near her ear. "If you do anything to embarrass me, I promise you will regret it."

She closed her eyes briefly as she thought of all the things she had done recently that would cause him embarrassment. It was on the tip of her tongue to tell him about her lost virtue but, despite his betrayal, she wouldn't endanger Gray needlessly. Jean could kill him.

"Here." The bouquet of white roses was pushed callously into her hands.

She gripped them instinctively to keep them from falling. Before she could respond, the front door opened. Her breath stopped and she thought, now, surely now her knight would come. But it was an older man she recognized from the Nelsons' ball. Jean left her to greet him and she heard his explanation of a late train, but then all sound stopped, at least for her, because Gray appeared in the entryway behind the new arrival.

He consumed her, leaving room for nothing else.

He had come! Their eyes met as he stepped around the guest and her uncle and came toward her. She took in a slow, shallow breath, afraid to hope, afraid to think that maybe now...maybe now he had come to save her. He was close enough that his scent assailed her, the leather and spice that clung to him, but also that scent she knew as his alone because she'd pressed her face against his naked flesh and breathed it in.

He walked by, close enough to touch. Near enough that the heat from his body reached out to her with airy tendrils that just barely brushed her. Yet, he did not stop. He simply kept walking until he stood in front of Monsieur Sinclair, his back to her. He'd gone by without even acknowledging her in any way. Her gaze took in the breadth of his back, the dark hair that fell past his shoulders and she remembered the solid strength of him beneath her hands, the silk of him between her fingers.

It couldn't have meant nothing to him.

Whatever he was saying to Monsieur Sinclair was too low for her to hear, but she seriously doubted her ability to understand language at this point, anyway. She was all sensation and emotion. He turned toward the doors and she knew an insane need to talk to him just once. To remind him that she was there.

"Gray," the word escaped her lips in a faint, aching whisper.

She almost thought he wouldn't hear, but his hand stopped on the crystal doorknob. He'd heard. Her heart leaped with joy but then his fingers turned the knob and he disappeared into the room. Words could never have conveyed what his actions had so eloquently accomplished.

She was alone.

Chapter Twelve

Whatever might have been said after that door closed, Sophie wasn't aware of it. She existed there in a fog of her own misery, reeling from Gray's rejection, her mind turning in on itself as it attempted to insulate her from the pain. All she knew was that when next she happened to notice, Jean was standing before her pushing that bouquet into her hands again. The flowers must have fallen, because she looked down and saw perfect white petals sprinkled across the polished wood floor.

She wanted to take the bouquet, tried to move her fingers, but they wouldn't respond to her command so the flowers fell to the floor again. Jean stood above her, murmuring some threat, the whites of his eyes seeming to glow from his anger, but she couldn't understand the words. Could only barely feel his fingers where they pressed around her arm.

Whatever Jean saw in her face seemed to reassure him and he let her go. Sophie glanced around to find the hall deserted. Monsieur Sinclair and the last guest must have gone inside. Martine had disappeared. She was alone again. The thought had barely registered before Jean was sliding her hand through his arm and escorting her into the parlor.

It was filled with men. A few had brought their wives but most had come alone. She recognized a few from balls and dinners but the others were new faces. Without conscious thought, her gaze sought Gray. Even if she'd walked in with her eyes closed, she would've known where he stood. She gravitated to him like iron to a magnet.

He stood against the wall to her left and watched her. She'd expected the cool demeanor he'd shown in the hall but his body was tense and his gaze burned into her. Even now, when he'd clearly abandoned her and she knew he felt nothing, those gray eyes had the power to touch her. She blinked to keep her composure and forced herself to stare straight ahead.

Jean had guided her to the end of the aisle where Anton stood waiting. She didn't acknowledge him, though, simply continued to stare ahead. Maybe if she kept herself away from what was taking place it wouldn't really happen. Maybe it would all go away and she would wake up back in Gray's room with his arms around her and his heart beating beneath her ear.

That was a foolish thought. She had no one but herself now.

Her only choice was to fight this marriage herself. Anger surged in her chest. She would turn around and tell everyone in this room that she objected to this marriage. Jean might still force her, but at least every one of them would have to deal with their guilty consciences. They would know that she was unwilling.

A glimmer of hope sparked that anger, bringing it to full, blazing life. She closed her eyes to draw courage from it and dropped her bouquet, closing her hands into fists, readying herself to fight her way out if necessary.

Anton's smarmy face came into focus when she opened them. He smiled at her, already anticipating having her to himself. Well, she wouldn't make it easy for him.

She opened her mouth to tell him no, but a voice louder than hers took over the entire room.

"Now!" The voice boomed. It might have been Monsieur Sinclair.

She turned her head to find him and saw the parlor doors had opened. Had someone else come in?

Monsieur Sinclair had withdrawn his gun and it was pointed right at Jean. He didn't look like a gunslinger anymore. His eyes were narrowed on her uncle and authority draped around him like an invisible cloak. "Jean LaSalle, you are under arrest."

For a split second the very air stilled, as if the room itself had drawn a breath.

Then everyone seemed to move at once.

Something hit her from behind so hard it laid her out on the ground and knocked the breath from her lungs. Men shouted but their words were lost to the roaring in her ears. The yells were accompanied by three gunshots in rapid succession followed by silence.

The room filled with the acrid smoke of the shots. It was so thick that it was bitter on her tongue. She tried to push up onto her knee but a heavy weight held her down. A man's hand rested on the floor next to her face. Gray's hand. She'd recognized it anywhere. His chest was against her back. He's the reason she was on the ground. He had tackled her and covered her with his body through the shooting.

The thought had barely registered before he shouted above her. He launched himself off of her, leaping on Anton who looked to be trying to get to his feet, but Gray tackled him. She watched in horror as they struggled, unable to comprehend what was going on. Her gaze took in the chaos of the room and saw that many others had come in; one of them she recognized as the sheriff, his star-shaped insignia pinned to his shirt. Monsieur Sinclair was kneeling near the door, his smoking gun still in hand.

She didn't see Jean, but Gray subdued Anton and left him lying on the floor with his hands tied behind his back. Over his inert form, she met Gray's quick glance and knew a moment of panic. He seemed a stranger to her, completely cold and remote as he focused on the task. She didn't know who he was. He clearly wasn't the man who had shared so much of himself with her, while simultaneously not sharing the most important part. The panic overwhelmed her, bringing her to her feet and making her run from the room and the confusion. She meant to run out the front door but it was wide open and there were even more men that way. So she turned and ran out the back. She didn't know where she hoped to run, only that she had to get away.

"Sophie!"

She'd barely cleared the back door when she heard Gray's voice. It spurred her forward toward the gate in the walled back-yard, but she didn't make it. He grabbed her just as her fingers were grasping to pull it open and dragged her back against him. Solid arms closed around her, but she refused to be subdued so easily and fought him.

"Why are you running? Sophie, stop fighting me!"

She went limp in his arms but only because she was still struggling to breathe. "What are you doing to me?" It was more a breathless plea than the furious question she'd meant it to be.

He buried his face in her hair, his lips warm against her ear. "Sophie." The tortured whisper burned as it rasped over the open wound of her heart.

His chest was so strong and solid against her back that she couldn't stop herself from reveling in it. She closed her eyes, causing tears to fall. It meant she was shameless and beyond any hope, but any chance she had to touch him was heaven to her and more than she could resist. And as his lips caressed her skin, she moved her head to give him better access to her neck. Only a moment more, she promised herself, only a moment to take with her for the rest of her life.

When he loosened his arms and moved a hand up to cup her face, she finally found the strength to pull away and bucked against him until she wrenched free and turned to face him. But he was persistent and grabbed her arms, pulling her close. Her hands settled on his chest and stayed there deadlocked.

"Don't look at me like that." His voice was hoarse. She was surprised to see the depth of pain in his eyes. "I can't bear that I hurt you."

She almost reached up to touch his face, to try to soothe the pain from his eyes, but then she remembered that *she* was the injured party. "You were going to let me get married," she accused.

"No! That never would've happened." To emphasize the words, he pulled her flush against him and his arms went around her. Sophie realized how useless her struggles had been, when she felt herself melting into him. "The wedding wasn't supposed to happen, but for the latecomers it wouldn't have got as far as it did. We'd hoped to arrest them before you even came downstairs, but LaSalle was determined to move things on as quickly as possible and we didn't have a chance. I hate like hell that you were there. I didn't think Sinclair would let you come in."

"Who are you, Gray? I don't understand what happened."

"LaSalle, Beaudin, and a few others were supposed to be arrested. Sinclair's been following them for years. They've been buying up land with mining potential, usually by forcing people to sell. He's murdered some of them. There's a whole slew of charges, but the wedding was an opportunity to get them all here in one place."

"Who are you?" she asked again, needing to know that more than anything else.

"Everything I told you I was." He spoke slowly, his gaze holding strong to hers. "Sinclair and Brand are deputy marshals. Cole and I are just helping out for the reward money and because I owe Sinclair a favor."

"So you let me go all this time thinking I had to marry that monster?" She watched him swallow.

"I know. Be angry." His fingertips touched her cheek. She pulled away, not yet willing to be placated and he let her go, his hand dropping to his side. He didn't step back, however, leaving only inches between them. "I wanted to tell you, but I couldn't. We couldn't take the chance." His gaze searched hers, looking for redemption.

She couldn't swallow past the lump that had lodged itself in her throat.

"Whatever else you think of me, Sophie, know this: I had decided you weren't marrying Beaudin, no matter what happened today."

"When did you decide that?"

"I think I knew it that day outside LaSalle's study when you first told me. There's no way I could let you go to him. I wouldn't have done it."

She believed him. The truth of his words moved through her like a balm, soothing every scrape and tear of the last month, maybe her entire life. She still found it difficult to reconcile the Gray she knew now, the one who had been on her side all along, to the Gray she had known then. The one she had come to love despite the fact that he worked for her uncle. Perhaps she had seen the truth of him all along.

He bridged the slight distance between them and reached for her slowly, giving her time to refuse him as he took her head in his hands. His fingers slid into her hair and curled, tugging it slightly in a way that made her scalp tingle. "Maybe you hate me now and I have no right to do this."

His questioning gaze searched hers until he moved so close, his eyes closed and his lips covered hers. He kissed her with all of the pent-up longing of the past two weeks. The second his tongue brushed her lips, she surrendered to his kiss and the yearning it stirred deep within her. Her arms went around his shoulders, so there wasn't a breath of space between them from breast to hip. And the kiss evolved into a heated, breathing thing of redemption and desire until he was drinking salvation from her lips. Finally he released her mouth, but still held her close with his forehead pressed to hers.

"When I watched you sleep that night, I knew I needed to

keep you safe. When you walked away from me in the morning, I hated myself for hurting you. I never want to cause you pain, Sophie." He closed his eyes and kissed the corner of her mouth and her brow before letting his arms drop and putting space between them again.

The action sobered her. She felt bereft suddenly without the comfort of his embrace. When he spoke, his voice was still gentle, but his tone was all business. "You should know that your uncle was shot pretty bad." He took a breath as if forcing himself to say what he needed to say. "I doubt he'll make it." His brow knitted, as if he expected censure.

She tried but she couldn't find any sadness. Jean had done terrible things to many people. "He died as he lived," was all she could manage to say. "I don't blame you for that."

"Thank you." Relief softened his features. "Beaudin can't buy himself out of the mess he's in, so he won't be a problem for you anymore. You'll be free now."

But not free of him. She opened her mouth to say something, but nothing would come out. Did he want to be with her? Was this his goodbye? She couldn't tell.

Finally, she managed to voice a portion of what she wanted. "What of you?"

"I'll find Alexandre for you," he said without hesitation.

"And that's it?" She held her breath locked tight in her throat.

He was silent, but she saw the struggle behind his eyes, saw his breath become heavy and his jaw tighten. "What more do you want? You can have anything. Everything."

Only in that moment did she understand that he was as wary as she, half-expecting rejection, hopeful for more.

"I want you." She breathed the words. "Only you."

His expression cracked, and he said, "You already have me, Sophie."

The breath she was holding came out as a sob and she moved forward to hold him. Her fingers tangled in his hair as she raised his tortured gaze to meet hers. "I love you, mon coeur."

Gray's arms wrapped tight around her hips and she squealed as he lifted her off her feet, holding her above him. "Then you're mine. I won't let you go."

She laughed as she slid down his body until she could kiss him. "Always, mon amour. Always."

Epilogue

It wasn't as difficult to find her brother as Sophie had expected. After that awful shootout, the authorities, led by Deputy Marshal Sinclair and the Sheriff, spent several hours going through Jean's papers to look for more evidence of the people he might have harmed. They left with boxes of files, promising to return them as soon as their case against Jean had been settled.

Finally, after everyone left—everyone but Gray—she conducted her own search of Jean's study. It turned out he had been corresponding with Alexandre, after all. Her brother wasn't in Chicago, but in Boston attending college. Judging from the letters, Alexandre believed that she was happily spending her days as a Society debutante. He hadn't been told about the marriage.

In response to her telegram the next day, he had taken a leave from his studies and come home that very week. Jean never made it through surgery, which meant most of the blame fell to Beaudin who had been right there with her uncle as he intimidated and bullied people to sign over their land. Together, she and Alexandre spent the next weeks putting their lives back together, while trying to return everything that had been stolen back to its rightful owners. As heirs of the property, it was theirs to do with as they wanted.

Through it all, Gray was beside her. He kissed her awake every morning and held her as she slept every night. He shared meals with them and offered his advice when asked. In short, he was everything she had ever dreamed of.

Sophie drew her shawl around her shoulders to keep out the cool, evening air as she leaned against the porch railing. Monsieur Sinclair was in town and had joined them for dinner, bringing with him the good news that Anton had pleaded guilty, confessing to his crimes in hopes of a lighter sentence. After celebrating the news enthusiastically, she had left them to their brandy so that she could get some fresh air.

She wasn't surprised to feel Gray's arms come around her. She closed her eyes and leaned back into him, loving the feeling of home he gave her. He pressed a soft kiss to her temple.

"You ran off too fast." He mildly chastised her.

"Too fast? Was I supposed to wait?"

He rifled in his pocket and then put his hand in front of her. A diamond ring on the end of his smallest finger glittered in the moonlight.

She gasped.

"Marry me?"

She grabbed his hand and then turned in his arms. "Gray?"

He grinned. "I planned to ask you in front of Alexandre and Sinclair, but this is better."

"You want to marry me?"

"Yes. I want to spend the rest of my days with you. I would have asked you sooner, but I wanted...well, I waited until everything was settled because you had enough to concern yourself with."

She felt a smile stretch across her face as she imagined having him in her life forever.

"Yes, Gray, I'll marry you."

He lifted her in his arms and swung her around. Then he kissed her and let her feet drop back down to earth. Pulling back, he loosened the solitaire diamond from his finger and pushed it onto hers. It wasn't as extravagant as the one she had received from Anton, but it was more beautiful than any piece of jewelry she had ever owned. It was the only one that had ever been given to her in love.

"I love you, Sophie." His voice was deep and true, and though she had felt it a million times over, it was the first time he'd ever said those words to her.

She pulled him against her and remembered the words she had once spoken to him.

I'm sorry for what you've gone through, mon coeur. But I'm thankful for whatever has led you to me.

They were true for her as well.

No matter what had happened in her past, it had all led her to Gray, her heart.

Keep reading for a sneak peek at *The Copper Heir* the next book in The Gilded West series...

The Copper Heir

The Gilded West (book 1)

Emmaline Drake knew trouble when it walked through the door. Five years of serving drinks had taught her that only three kinds of strangers ever entered Jake's Saloon in the tiny backwater town of Whiskey Hollow. The first two were drifters and loners who sought the saloon as a refuge from a world that didn't accept them. They kept to themselves and rarely caused trouble. A drink, a meal and conversation with a pretty girl were enough to send them on their way. But then there were men like the three who stood just inside the saloon's swinging, slatted doors. These men were the third type and just looking at them caused a knot of dread to churn tight in her stomach.

These men were outlaws.

If there was anything Emmaline knew, it was how to spot an outlaw. Thanks to her stepfather's profession, she'd had years of experience identifying the variations in that type of man. As a rule they were notoriously badly dressed, though the clothing of this particular group belied that rule. Even with their dusters covered with a layer of trail dust, the fine cloth and texture of their trousers and coats were apparent and their boots were obviously high quality. But it wasn't the clothing that made the outlaw. It was the eyes. Outlaws had the eyes of predators—full of intensity and aggression.

Violence crackled like energy in the eyes of these men.

They paused to boldly survey the room and all conversation died. A wave of awareness sucked out the sound as it moved throughout the handful of tables, silencing the patrons and leaving tension in its wake. Even Lucy, Jake's wife, who'd been pounding away on the woefully out of tune piano in the corner, faltered and let her fingers fall still. No one overtly acknowledged the newcomers, unless you counted the sideways glances from behind hunched shoulders as the men in the room took note of them without shifting their positions. The customers were like dogs, bristling at potential intruders.

After taking note of every occupant in the room, they did another pass, no doubt noting the bare wood floors and rough edges of the place. Jake hadn't spent much money on making the saloon appealing. There was no need when the nearest competition was more than a two days' ride away.

Emmaline stood at the bar, her hands clenched on the scarred and polished wood. She swallowed as she watched them through the narrow, cracked mirror that hung behind it. It was framed in an elaborate plaster that had been gilded at one time, but most of it had long since chipped away, leaving it a mere ghost of its former self. She had thought many times that that was probably an apt description of the town itself. Once it had been a thriving mining community, but when the creek had been picked clean of gold, everyone had moved on.

Gesturing to Jake for three whiskeys, she turned to set eyes on the strangers. They were taller than the mirror had suggested and meaner looking. The quality of their clothing struck her again. Their trousers weren't patched with the leather that sometimes adorned the thighs of the men who spent most of their time in the saddle. They were tailored, not the simple clothing of ranchers and cowhands.

Even their coats were a thick wool that would have made her envious if she hadn't been so busy trying not to be afraid. They were no ordinary outlaws. These weren't the same type of men she'd known in her stepfather's gang. These men exuded power along with danger, a dark intent that said it was no accident that they had found their way to the saloon on that particular night. They were on the hunt and every man in this room had something to hide. It was a combination that could turn deadly with only the slightest provocation.

Each of them was over six feet tall, but the one on the right towered over the others by a few inches. He wasn't the least bit gaunt as often happened with tall men, as if they couldn't possibly eat enough food to support such a build. His powerful frame matched his height and his black eyes blazed with fury as he boldly looked over everyone in the room, sizing each of them up for the threat they might present and then discarding them one by one. It was hard to imagine the man who could pose a threat to him. An angry red scar ripped down his cheek and contributed to his fierce appearance, but he would've had no problems carrying out the look without it.

The middle one had thick black hair, a furrowed brow, and appeared just as fierce as his partner, but more measured and calm. Less brute power, despite his broad shoulders and thick chest. His vivid green eyes were alight with intelligence and intensity, and he exuded an autocratic air that left her willing to bet anything that he was the leader.

But it was the one on the left who drew her attention and held it. With his physique, he could've been a match for the leader, except that his hair was lighter, that indefinable shade that hovered between rich brown and golden blond. He had a square chin with the hint of an indentation and a full, sculpted bottom lip. He seemed almost lazily indifferent, except that his eyes carried a calculating intensity that held her momentarily rooted to the floor when he happened to glance her way. A bolt of awareness shot directly to her belly as their eyes met, sending her pulse soaring and making her look away quickly as if she'd been caught doing something sinful.

The giant of a man walked to a table near the door and the other two followed suit, moving with caution, clearly suspicious of everyone else. The dark blond one on the left moved with surprising grace for a man of his strength, like he knew the full power of his body and knew how to control it. Somehow, observing that made her more aware of her own body and exactly how much of her breasts were on display. The realization made her blush.

"Em?" Jake's voice penetrated the strange fog that had come over her.

"Yeah?"

Eyebrows raised and his tanned brow furrowed, he nodded to the three drinks on the tray beside her.

Always sensible and rarely flustered, she shook off the inexplicable fog that had come over her and grabbed the discolored tin tray with both hands.

"Be careful." Because she knew him well, she could easily discern the grimace lurking behind the caterpillar moustache that obliterated any hint of a mouth. But it was the nervous gesture of his hand running through his graying hair that ratcheted her anxiety up a level. He was always calm, even on that night two years ago when that bank robber had come in and everyone had recognized him from the flyer hanging beside the door. Jake had merely grabbed the short-barreled shotgun he kept behind the bar and offered the man a chance to leave. He had taken it.

Unable to stifle the impulse in time, she turned her head to look at the billboard postings. There were five posters there, but none of the drawings resembled the strangers. Of course, two of them were drawings of men with kerchiefs covering the lower halves of their faces, so there was always the possibility.

"Do you know them?" she whispered and turned her attention back to Jake.

He shook his head, but his eyes shifted to their table again. "No, but I have my suspicions. Go on now. We'll talk later."

How was she supposed to remain composed when he went and said something like that? Now that the men had settled themselves at a table, the conversations resumed and the tension in the room decreased notably. Lucy even resumed her piano playing, but at a more sedate pace. Her own anxiety should have begun to abate, but it hadn't, her stomach refused to stop its churning and she couldn't shake the feeling that something was terribly wrong. That something dangerous and profound was about to happen and she was powerless to stop it, like being stuck on a runaway train that was about to run out of track and she could only hold on and watch as it flew over the edge of a cliff.

With Jake's warning spinning around in her mind, Emmaline tightened her grip on the tray and slowly made her way to the table. She'd long ago become accustomed to the revealing nature of her outfit, but as she approached, she longed for the modest dresses she wore every day on the farm. The costume she wore at the saloon had been one of her mother's gowns from her days in the brothel in Helena. Emmaline and her sisters had modified it by shortening the deep red silk to knee-length and adding two layers of black lace taken from another gown. The bodice had already been obscenely low, so they had only had to add the matching black lace there. It revealed a large amount of her cleavage with its nonexistent sleeves, mere scraps of fabric that dropped low off her shoulders to hang down her upper arms. Her legs at least were covered in sensible black, woolen stockings. She'd started out with her mother's silk ones, but they had worn out years ago. She'd always disliked the costume, but never more so than now as she walked toward a table full of outlaws.

She shivered as she approached the doorway. Though the days were getting warmer, winter had refused to relinquish its grip on the nights. The other customers were drinking and keeping warm at tables near the cast-iron stove that sat further inside, but not the strangers. Apparently they preferred to keep their distance, as if she needed any further proof of their dubious intentions.

As she advanced, the pretty one with light hair—is that how she was referring to him?—turned the full force of his gaze on her. It licked its way up her legs and over her hips, settling on her breasts for a moment before finally making its way to her face. He'd sat back in his chair, one leg stretched out before him, almost lazy in his regard of her. She had worked at the saloon for almost five years, so she was used to the looks men gave her. She even encouraged them in the hopes that those passing through would leave a little extra on the table for her—the locals had nothing extra to leave. But with him...the look was different. It wasn't merely taking in what the dress put on display. His eyes demanded her attention, demanded her response, demanded much more than she was willing to give, while his lips promised more than she could risk imagining. One corner of his mouth turned upward, a suggestive smile that had her blushing again. Holy hell, what was happening to her? Men didn't affect her this way. She didn't allow it, because she knew they couldn't be trusted.

Tearing her gaze away from him, she focused her attention safely on the scarred, wooden tabletop as she sat the tray down and offered her customary greeting. "Welcome, gentlemen. Jake sends his regards."

"Jake?" The pretty one spoke, his voice a deep rumble that warmed her deep down in ways she refused to acknowledge.

"The owner." Without looking up, she gestured over her shoulder toward the bar where Jake stood watching...she hoped. Then she carefully set a tumbler with a finger of whiskey in front of each man. On the rare occasions Jake thought it necessary, he'd preemptively send over a free drink to welcome a new customer. If the man felt indebted or grateful to the proprietor, he'd be less likely to leave a mess behind. Sometimes it worked, sometimes it didn't.

The giant picked his up and tossed it back before she'd even finished.

"Rotgut." The hard voice matched its owner.

Glancing up, she met his disapproving look with a challenge in hers. "We don't serve rotgut, sir." She actually didn't know if that was true or not. Men complained that other saloons cut their whiskey, but nobody had ever complained about Jake's. She wouldn't put it past him, though. With the amount of business they'd had lately, it was barely worth her time to make the trip into town for work.

"My friend has expensive tastes." The pretty one pulled a wallet out of a pocket hidden inside his coat. It was a smooth, chocolate-colored leather with no creases, almost brand-new, she'd guess. When he opened it to extract a note, she could see many others nestled inside. The confident way he carried himself, along with his clothing, had left little doubt in her mind as to his wealth, but this only confirmed that she was right to be suspicious. What were they doing in Whiskey Hollow? Bringing trouble, she was certain of it. "A bottle of your finest Kentucky bourbon." His gaze licked over her and one corner of his mouth tipped up as he extended a ten-dollar note to her.

"We only have rye. Overholt?" The question forced her to look at him. She was struck anew by the strong, masculine beauty of his features. High wide cheekbones, strong granite jaw covered with a dusting of honeyed stubble, perfectly formed lips. This one was trouble in more ways than one.

He merely gave a single nod, indicating the substitution would be fine, and lifted an eyebrow when she hadn't taken the money.

Remembering herself, she grabbed the note, deliberately making sure to not touch him, and gave a small smile to the other two. They did not return her smile. "I'll be right back."

Emmaline managed to keep her steps even and measured all the way back to the bar. But when she placed the tray down, her gaze speared Jake where he stood. "They want a bottle of rye. Come to the back and help me get one."

He looked like he wanted to argue—she knew he kept a few bottles under the bar—but she needed to know what he knew of them. Some instinct warned her that their presence had something to do with her stepfather's absence. He and her older stepbrother, Pete, were over a week late coming home from their latest job, which wasn't entirely uncommon, but no one had heard from them. A hollow feeling in the pit of her stomach said that the job had gone terribly wrong. As much as she disagreed with their lifestyle, it turned her stomach to think of what would happen to her and her younger sisters without them.

"Who are they?" she asked the moment Jake stepped through the door to the tiny storeroom filled with crates of bottled beer and barrels of moonshine. "Does their presence have anything to do with Ship?" Though he was her stepfather, everyone called him Ship, even her younger sisters who were his blood.

"Calm down, Em." He placed a hand on her shoulder. "I don't know anything for sure and getting upset won't help anything. You've heard of the Reyes Brothers? That could be them. That one in the middle, the one that looks like a Spaniard, he's Reyes and I think he's their leader."

The Reyes Brothers. A chill prickled her scalp and cold ribbons of fear trailed down her spine. Ship had talked about them the last time he'd been home. Though she hadn't gotten the impression the two had crossed paths, he'd described the successes of the gang with the glee and admiration only someone hoping to rise to those levels could summon. They moved cattle across the border. Lots of cattle. Which was only illegal depending on which side of the border they were on. But to hear Ship tell it, they'd made a fortune guarding mining and land claims and even that wasn't technically illegal, unless it involved killing. She couldn't remember anything else he'd said. The only detail she'd taken to heart from that conversation was that no one crossed them and lived to tell about it.

Had Ship done something stupid like try to steal from them? Had he taken Pete with him?

"That doesn't make sense. They work down near the border. Las Cruces, or was it Santa Fe? Damn, I can't remember. Why would they be here?"

Jake shrugged. "My buddy down off Green River swears he saw Reyes there last month buying supplies. He'd know because he spent some time near the border just last year. Says he was in a saloon down in Perez and in he walked with a giant, I suppose that one he brought with him tonight. Both better dressed than normal outlaws. He walked in and called out to a fella playing faro. The man charged him with his gun drawn so they shot him. Reyes left and the giant followed him out. No one said a word and the poor son of a bitch was carted out the back and his winnings divided amongst those at the table." He ran a hand over the back of his neck and glanced at the closed door leading to the bar. "Seems like if they were in Green River last month they could be here now. It's not that far away."

"Is this the same buddy you have to carry out every time he comes in because he drinks an entire jar of moonshine?" When he gave an irritated sigh, confirming her words, she continued, "That man could be anybody."

"Sure he could, but how often do you see men dressed like that step foot in here?"

Not many passed through here if they could help it, not since all the mines had been bought out and the creek picked clean of gold, and certainly none dressed like those men. They were here for a reason. "Do you think they're looking for Ship? Is he hiding?"

"I don't know, Em. I wish I could say. I haven't heard a word from him. Just go back out there and act as if nothing's wrong. You don't know anything."

Grabbing a bottle of Old Overholt—how anyone could drink it, she didn't know—she gave Jake a quick nod and headed back out. A small part of her had hoped they'd left, but there they sat, deep in discussion about something. Perhaps their next murder.

Jake followed her out and placed three fresh tumblers on her tray. He gave her a nod of encouragement and then she was off to the lion's den. She kept her gaze down the entire walk over, unwilling to lock eyes with the pretty one again. If she could just get through this, then she could prove to the knot in her belly that nothing was wrong, that nothing had happened to Ship and Pete.

Without a word, she sat the tray down on the table and unloaded the bottle and three fresh tumblers, before retrieving the tray and turning to go. It was easy, simple. There was absolutely no reason to believe that these men meant her any harm. The pretty one had actually smiled at her earlier. And she knew that smile. He wanted to do something, but it didn't involve hurting her. Quite the opposite, in fact. Everything was fine.

But then the leader reached out and put a hand on her arm, his long, tapered fingers curling gently around her wrist. "A moment, please." His voice was soft and quiet, commanding respect from the confidence and intensity of the tone rather than the volume. Though his grip was gentle, she could feel the strength he held in check.

She followed the length of his arm up to his face, afraid to hear his next words. But he held silent, waiting for her to meet his gaze. When she did, she was startled to realize his eyes were the exact odd shade of greenish-gold as the pretty one's. They were striking against his darker complexion. Could the two be related?

"Yes?"

"Tell us what you know of Ship Campbell."

Get your copy of *The Copper Heir* by Harper St. George

Also by Harper St. George

Visit my website for a complete list of books. ◻
https://www.harperstgeorge.com

The Gilded West

The Runaway Heiress (novella)
The Copper Heir
The Bastard Heir
The Gilded Lady

The Doves of New York

The Stranger I Wed

THE RUNAWAY HEIRESS

Eliza and the Duke

The Gilded Age Heiresses

The Heiress Gets a Duke
The Devil and the Heiress
The Lady Tempts an Heir
The Duchess Takes a Husband

Sons of Sigurd

Falling for Her Viking Captive

To Wed a Viking

Marrying Her Viking Enemy
Longing for Her Forbidden Viking

Viking Warriors

Enslaved by the Viking
One Night with the Viking
In Bed with the Viking Warrior
The Viking Warrior's Bride

Blood and Glory

HARPER ST. GEORGE

Dirty Boxing
Take Down
No Contest

About the author

Harper St. George was raised in the rural backwoods of Alabama and along the tranquil coast of northwest Florida. It was a setting filled with stories of the old days that instilled in her a love of history, romance, and adventure. By high school, she had discovered the historical romance novel which combined all of those elements into one perfect package. She has been hooked ever since.

She lives in the Atlanta area with her family. She would love to hear from you. Visit her website to sign up for her newsletter at www.harperstgeorge.com/newsletter and connect with her on social media.